Summer
Situations

Summer Situations

Three Novellas

Ann Birstein

This is a work of fiction. Names, characters, places, events, and incidents either are the product of the author's imagination or are used fictitiously. Any resemblance to actual persons, living or dead, businesses, companies, events, or locales is entirely coincidental.

Love in the Dunes appeared originally in the Winter 1971 issue of *Mediterranean Review*.

Copyright © 1971, 1972 by Ann Birstein

Cover design by Neil Alexander Heacox

ISBN: 978-1-5040-0845-7

Distributed in 2015 by Open Road Distribution
345 Hudson Street
New York, NY 10014
www.openroadmedia.com

To Kate

Contents

Summer
Situations

Love in the Dunes

THE ROOM in which Mrs. Kane lay breathing rapidly was like the inside of a ship, all timbered and beamed with varnished faintly creaking wood, and filled with slightly damp easy chairs and lamps whose nautical shades were tilted at pleasantly odd angles. Directly in front of her was a long sliding window open to the night and through it she could hear the distant lapping of the surf and see a perfectly round moon scudding through the clouds. Behind her a dog snuffled sweetly at the fire. A moment, a place of utter peace. But nevertheless Mrs. Kane lay breathing rapidly. For it had just dawned on her, it had just lit up her mind like a pitch-black tree pierced by lightning, that Charlie Krebs was the one. She grabbed convulsively at a pack of cigarettes in her lap, lit one and began to pace the room.

Why Charlie Krebs? she asked herself. Why me? Why now? The trouble was that she knew the answers to all these questions, for even as a girl she had been a competent amateur psychologist. This was what had made her so unpopular with boys, and later so attractive to men. All the boys ever wanted to do was neck, but men, she discovered later, love nothing better than a woman who explains things to them, and even her own husband Max still looked at her with tears of gratitude when she told him gently that he really wanted to dominate his mother. The real question was, did she actually want to know the answer? Wouldn't it be better, wouldn't it be wonderful for the first time to sink in deeper than any analysis, to dive down and down and down with her hair streaming up behind her and no hope of touching bottom? Mrs. Kane was a terrible swimmer; she went in up to her armpits and then puffed and chugged around pretending, if someone were watching, that she was keeping an eye on the children, any children. But she still thought of life, life lived to the fullest, as going into water over your head. And someday she intended to do just that. Perhaps even tomorrow if it were a good day for the beach. But this was not the point right now. Irritated with herself, Mrs. Kane pitched her cigarette into the fire and brought her mind back to the problem at hand.

Now where was she before she wandered off? Oh, yes, with Charlie. Darling Charlie—she permitted herself a dopey smile and a sigh. Holding hands with Charlie and sinking deeper and deeper and deeper while the water lapped at their slippery skins. She closed her eyes and for a moment the sensation was so real she got goose pimples. It was the goose pimples that decided her against the whole thing. No, no, it was one thing to daydream about Charlie idly while everyone was out for a walk and quite another to have such a vivid picture of his bare skin. She was ashamed of herself now for thinking that she had any choice with Charlie but to analyze him right out of existence. It would be a little disappointing perhaps—even this moment there were pangs and twinges—but in the end she would have done herself a great favor. The same kind of favor she had been offering all her friends in need over the years. Like poor Marjorie that weekend they were away in the country and Marjorie had come running to her for advice about the waiter. Oddly enough, the waiter had really meant it when he said he wanted to marry Marjorie, and now ten years had passed since Marjorie became Mrs. Rosenzweig and stopped speaking to her. A curious turn of events, and how time did fly. But never mind. If she were Marjorie she would have no hesitation what to do. She would sit her down in the big wing chair by the fire—she sat herself down in the big wing chair by the fire—and talk to her, kindly of course, but straight from the shoulder. Marjorie, she would say, now let us be honest with ourselves. Firstly, aside from the fact that Charlie Krebs is your husband's friend and colleague and that they both teach in the same department, you don't even like Charlie Krebs in the wintertime. It's just that here you are at the beach and the summer always makes everything seem possible. Mrs. Kane winced at other things that other summers had made seem possible. No, Marjorie, she resumed in a somewhat sterner tone, during the academic year Charlie Krebs is as nothing to you. Just another instructor working on his PhD in his spare time, and something of a lecher at that. And his clothes, those sleazy flapping suits and pointy shoes. Even his socks have clocks on them. To say nothing of the fact that he's always hanging around your kitchen looking so hungry you end up inviting him to dinner. It's Marlene who's your real friend, Marlene, his *wife*, remember? Which is why with the women getting along so well, you're all up here sharing this house in the first place. And now you want to spoil it all just for the sake of a passing fancy. Right, Marjorie? Right!

Mrs. Kane nodded and lit another cigarette. Propping up her bare feet on the dog's gently rising and falling back, she looked into the fire. The logs were blazing up, drawing all the light out of the room and giving everything, the dog, her feet, the driftwood on the mantelpiece, a dark philosophical cast. She felt like someone in a Dickens novel who had blundered out of a snowstorm into a deserted inn. Brooding, firelit thoughts came to her as she waited for her joint and ale. For instance, if Marjorie were really there would she have let her off so lightly just now? Never. Once Marjorie was on the mat, she would have spread-eagled her. She would have driven home the point that it wasn't even Charlie Krebs that made her blood run hot and cold, but time. Yes, time that old thief who loved to put sweet nothings in his book and close it. A sardonic smile flitted across her face. Come, my lass, facts is facts. Here you are, twenty-nine teetering on the brink of thirty, and—why not admit it?—for months now you've been looking for all the heartache you used to think would come to you in the natural course of events. So you pick on poor Charlie Krebs. But it's *life* that's really ailing you. Everybody's life—after all, you're a feeling girl—but especially your own life in Gorham. Mrs. Kane paused uneasily. She had not even thought of Gorham for weeks now, ever since they had all left it for this nautical hideaway, but now it sprang full-blown and unbidden into her head. Fixing her eyes on the fire—my god, she really was straight out of Dickens—it all came back to her with sickening clarity: the bright green campus, the white steeple, three hatchet-faced ladies marching off to a faculty tea, a tattered copy of Dr. Spock lying on somebody's floor, a football coach slapping her on the back at a cocktail party and telling her to get with it. Mrs. Kane shuddered and quickly turned into Marjorie again. Poor Marjorie, she thought, poor dear Marjorie. Someday life in Gorham will kill you. Or if not Gorham (Max had no tenure yet) then some other quaint college town exactly like it. It will be like jumping into a full-color page of *Life* magazine and knocking your brains out. What a way to go. She shook her head mournfully. You know, Marjorie, if you want to know the truth, my heart bleeds for you. Especially when I consider that only a moment ago—after all, what's a few years in eternity?—you could have been anything you set your mind to, a première danseuse, a playwright, maybe even the first woman conductor. And now here you sit, just awakening to the fact that you're chained down on every side, with a car and a husband and a baby and that goddamned heat bill. It was the heat bill that pushed Mrs. Kane over the edge. She leaped to her feet furiously. Was it for this you majored in English? she cried. Was it for this you wrote papers on the heroic couplet? *No, no, a thousand times no!* Marjorie slunk away, in search of a better life presumably, which left Mrs. Kane quite alone again.

So that was that. How ironic. And soon the three of them, Max and Marlene and Charlie, would wander back, never guessing what mad passions had surged up and been vanquished in their absence. The dog made a sad mewing sound, like a cat. Mrs. Kane patted him consolingly before starting off again for her couch by the window. Oh, well, there were other consolations, she thought, stretching out and squinting at the moon and wispy clouds, such as this brief moment of solitude after almost three weeks of finding people and children behind every door. She wasn't complaining. You expected that kind of thing when you shared a house, counting eggs at breakfast, conclaves at the bathroom door, finding all the good chairs taken when you wanted to read a book. Her only real surprise, almost a shock you might say, was seeing Charlie Krebs—good old Charlie Krebs, she thought with a faint stab of bitterness—turn into a ravishing sunburned Adonis the minute he hit the beach. Those legs of his. She had never seen such long tan legs in her life. She lifted her own leg and arched her instep thoughtfully, wondering why she suddenly had a marvelous creeping sensation that she was being observed and admired in every pore. How funny if Charlie should come walking in by himself now. And finding her alone—but no, she had promised not to think about Charlie anymore. Only it was so hard, right now even excruciating, since every picture of him that flashed through her mind was more enticing than the last. Oh, that lean limber body. The way he sat by the fire in the evening calmly smoking a pipe. Charlie resting his hand against the mast of a rented sailboat as if he owned it, before stripping off his shirt and diving into the water like a clean slender fish. Charlie. . . .

"Come on, Shirley," he had murmured before they all set off that evening. "Come walk with us."

"I don't want to," she had answered coldly.

"Why not, don't you like to walk?"

"Naturally, I like to walk. It's only that tonight, tonight I want—" She had given him a stricken look, and there it was. The thought that had been rapping at her brain for days had finally gained entrance. Well, why not? Take a running leap off the deck with Charlie and be done with it. But wait. Suppose Charlie didn't want to? She had to smile at her own foolishness. It was not only that Charlie always chased her into the pantry at parties in Gorham, and that out of everyone who ever chased her only Charlie caught her. There were other recent signs. Like an unexpected finger passed slowly down her bare back, or that Fourth of July kiss that Max, entering the room unexpectedly, had interrupted with a cough, or that curiously thrilling smile he had given her just before he went out the door tonight, the smile that made her feel as if an electric current had just shot through her. She tightened her body into a hard little knot. Please, please Charlie, come back and smile at me again. Run across the room on those beautiful long legs of yours and throw yourself on the couch beside me and—no, no, *no*, she thought desperately, I mustn't, I mustn't. We're all so happy here, and the children get along fine, and Marlene and I don't fight in the kitchen. It would be madness to spoil it. I have to be rational. I have to remember it's only proximity or geography or something statistical. I mean, what else can I expect when he's the last thing I see at night and the first thing in the morning? And then it's just that Max and I—well it *has* been five years in that same lousy bed, and he does sit like a lump on the beach, and also even this winter I told Marlene Krebs I had a horrible feeling I was going to have an affair with someone soon. She had lurched over on her side, pressing her hot face against the wall like a child with a fever, when suddenly the door creaked open.

"Shirley? Shirley?" This was Max.

"Sh," Charlie whispered, "she's asleep." Charlie, Charlie, do you care if I'm sleeping? Would you come near and stroke my hair if you could?

"She'll be uncomfortable there all night," Max said sternly.

"No, she won't," Marlene Krebs said, "it's a nice dumpy old couch."

Reluctantly, Max let himself be ushered away. There were loud tiptoeings across the board floor. Mrs. Kane lay perfectly still all the while, pretending to sleep so well that soon she did. The last thing she felt was the hand of Max, poor Max, covering her with a blanket.

Two brown half-naked children stood beside her bed, a puddle by the feet of one of them, Charlie Krebs's little boy. Shirley Kane closed her eyes fretfully. Now, how was she supposed to feel romantic about a man whose son wasn't toilet trained? "Honestly, Max," she said, "you'd think, wouldn't you that—?" But the bed crammed next to hers in the summer cardboard bedroom was empty. Where in the world was Max? Was he now lying on the couch in the sea-blown sunny living room? She remembered jumping up from the couch sometime toward morning, trailing her blanket after her and stripping and falling into her own bed. Had Max, waking suddenly and propelled by some automatic desire, taken off after her, and not finding her, simply fallen asleep in her place? She was tired of these dim nocturnal wanderings. Two little moles groping after each other the whole night long. And no telling where they would wind up in the morning. It would make any person uneasy to find when he awoke that he had to reconstruct the whole night before. There was a loud clatter of dishes from the kitchen. No, Max was probably already having breakfast. It was later than she had realized. Looking out the window she saw the sun clean white already and the glistening sparse sandy grass. Charlie Krebs's voice boomed out from somewhere.

"Where the hell are those kids?"

The voice was absolutely wonderful, deep, masculine, energetic. It had been one of the most delightful surprises of her life to see how Charlie Krebs behaved in the morning, so quick and authoritative in his movements. By now it was the custom for her and Marlene to sleep a little later than the others and usually by the time they came into breakfast Charlie would already have the children lined up on one side of the table, his son and daughter and her little girl, in size places, like little ducks in a shooting gallery.

"Go on, children," she whispered brightly. "Hurry up now." To Billy Krebs standing by his puddle, she added, "Your daddy's waiting."

Billy Krebs stared at her and blinked.

"Chluph," said her own little girl.

Oh, well, Mrs. Kane thought, his can't pee straight but mine can't talk, and he's one little girl ahead of me. So I suppose that makes us even. "Go on, go on, children," she whispered again, giving them a gentle little shove, and having made sure they had really trotted off, jumped out of bed, avoiding the wet spot on the floor just in time, and hurried into her shorts and blouse. Grabbing her comb and lipstick, she peered out of the door quickly to make sure there was no one around and then made a dash for the bathroom. What a difference a day made, she thought, washing her face and brushing her teeth, even a day in which nothing had happened except in her mind. Yesterday she would have thought nothing of wandering into breakfast any old way, probably with bare feet and in her pink cotton bathrobe. Yet today here she was darting furtively about the corridors making sure no one would see her until she was fit to be seen. She carefully dried her face, observing that it was getting tanner and tanner every day with hardly a spot of peel except on the nose, a triumphant answer to all those busybodies who warned her to get out of the sun. Then she swept her hair to one side—it was bleached almost blond now—and wound it in a long thick braid hanging over one shoulder. A bit too dramatic, too startlingly unlike her? Well, why not? It was the summer after all. Anything goes. Next a touch of eyebrow pencil, unfortunately her eyebrows had bleached too, almost to the point of invisibility, and then a gay abandoned smear of lipstick, pink and shiny against her tan skin. She sucked in her cheeks and looked at herself from under half-closed eyelids.

"My name is Tond-e-*ley*-o," she murmured. And then, despite herself, "King of Kings." The hell with it. She was hungry.

In the kitchen the three ducklings sat all in a row, slurping their cereal from identical red plastic bowls. Charlie, as usual, had arranged them very neatly, and with the sunlight glancing off their intent golden heads they were a radiant little trio. It pleased her to think that all children were born blond nowadays, and that she had not seen a black-haired child or a kinky-haired child, or for that matter, a cross-eyed child in many years. Charlie was fair. Max was dark.

"Good *morning*, angels," she said, and then, sinking down on a kitchen chair, "Good morning, Charlie."

"Coffee?" Charlie asked.

"Oh *would* you? You're a darling."

She had avoided looking at Charlie Krebs until this moment, but now feeling the heat of him behind her with the coffee pot, she could no longer contain herself. Turning quickly, she met him head on. His eyeglasses dazzled her—an old weakness of hers, she suddenly remembered, tall men with glasses. "Hi," she whispered.

"Hi." Quickly, before the children had time to look up from their cereal, Charlie bent and kissed her ear. The electric shock went through her. Her ear burned. Oh, Charlie, Charlie, did you just feel what I felt? Is it the same for you as it is for me? Oh, Charlie, what shall we *do*? Half-swooning with delight, she took the cup of coffee from him and set it on the table with a trembling hand. Suddenly her legs were soaking wet. After one moment of horror she realized it was her daughter Sally who had just climbed off her stool, pattered around the table, and solemnly poured out a glass of ice-cold milk into her mother's lap.

"Goddamn it, Sally!" Mrs. Kane cried, leaping up from her chair. She grabbed the baby's wrist. "Now, Sally, you know perfectly well you're not supposed to do that. It's not funny at all. It's not even cute."

"Chluph?" Sally said inquiringly."

"And stop pretending you don't understand me. Not talking is one thing. Not understanding is another. And I happen to know perfectly well that—"

Across the table, Billy Krebs began to cry. Then Betsy. It was amazing how she kept forgetting all about Betsy Krebs, perhaps because Betsy was five and went for long solitary walks.

"Now stop it, Betsy. You're older. Try to be reasonable. And you too, Billy." Sally was wailing now too. The situation was really getting out of hand, except when you stopped to think about it Sally's face was much nicer when she was crying. "Oh, never mind," Mrs. Kane said, "just forget the whole thing." Turning to Charlie with what she hoped was a gay shrug, an indication that this was only the briefest hiatus in a great stream of pleasures, she asked him to save her coffee for her and dashed into the bedroom to change her shorts. Her only clean pair was bright blue and clashed hideously with her chartreuse blouse, but there was no choice. Then, as long as she was at it, she went off again to trap Sally, who was still wandering around in a long-sleeved pajama top and a bare behind. While Sally fought and hopped on one leg and then the other, she managed to cram her into a tiny pair of shorts and a T-shirt, but after one sneaker Sally was off again. Clutching the other sneaker, Mrs. Kane went after her, racing down the hall, into the bathroom, and in and almost out of the living room where Max looked up from an old copy of *Partisan Review* and nodded. He was frowning reflectively as if he had just read that the plight of the intellectual was even worse than he thought.

"Good morning, darling," Mrs. Kane said dutifully, with one foot out the door.

"What's your rush?" Max said. "Sit down and talk to me."

Mrs. Kane reluctantly drew her foot back in. "I was looking for Sally," she explained. "She's running around with one sneaker."

"Sally's outside with Billy. And just as well. If I were that child's parents, I wouldn't let him back in until he was housebroken."

"Now, now, Max," Mrs. Kane said, "no need to take on so." Ever since the other day when Max had sat down where Billy Krebs had been sitting, Max had been very edgy about the Krebs family.

"Take on so?" Max cried. "I'd like to know where the world would be if no one took on! Anyhow," he continued, subsiding a little and speaking with strained sweetness, "I should think most people would want to distinguish their children from the lower animals, wouldn't you? Or don't you mind that your friends consider themselves perpetual graduate students and therefore permanently relieved of all responsibility?"

"*My* friends?" Mrs. Kane said. "You're the one who found them."

"You slept on the couch last night," Max said.

"I know."

"I know you know. But that's not the way to get a good night's sleep."

"I know."

"I know you—oh, the hell with it. I can't even figure you out since you took up the beachcombing life."

Mrs. Kane cast a yearning look down the hall toward the kitchen where Charlie the darling was probably still keeping her coffee warm. Would it be safe to make a dash for it? Max had already picked up his magazine, slapped his stomach a couple of times, and begun to read absorbedly. Really, someday she must talk to him about the way he wore his shirt flopping loose over his Bermuda shorts, or for that matter the fact that he wore Bermuda shorts at all. The real trouble with Max, she decided, was that he was a good five years older than the rest of them and also had been married before, for six months to a frivolous woman named Patsy. Since then Max had come to regard frivolity as a destroyer of marriages. Which wouldn't have been too bad except that more and more lately he was turning to the works of Thomas Carlyle. Naturally, next to Carlyle everyone else was bound to seem outrageously lighthearted. What a cross to bear. Other women had alcohol, she had *Sartor Resartus*. To Max, she said: "There's nothing to figure out. You're just imagining things as usual."

"Imagining things?" Max said, flipping over a page. "Then what about all these recitations lately of 'Gather ye rosebuds while ye may'? And that touching soliloquy yesterday about your college lover, what's his name—Gus."

"Gerald!" she shouted.

"Now what are you two bickering about?" Marlene Krebs said, sailing cool as a cucumber through the doorway.

"We never bicker. We argue. There's a difference," Max said, laying down his magazine. "Come here and sit on my lap. The sea air agrees with you."

"Certainly," Marlene said pleasantly.

Mrs. Kane looked at her closely. Max was right about her—unfortunately Max was often right—and it was something she should have taken into consideration the night before. The sea air was doing as much for Marlene as it was for Charlie. (A very outdoorsy couple, come to think of it.) Back in Gorham, what with her shelves full of canned goods, her children underfoot, and her unironed dirndl skirts, Marlene looked like the usual young academic Mother Hubbard. But living by the sea was making a queen of her. Even now, as she perched on Max's hairy knees, her back was straight and her lovely chin pointed high. Also, though she wore an old pair of denim shorts and a torn man's shirt—Charlie's?—she had coiled her black hair into a sleek, positively regal bun. How did she manage it all in the morning? Mrs. Kane wondered, feeling more and more like a Tootsie Roll bursting out of its wrapper.

"Well, what should we all do today?" Marlene said, patting the top of Max's bushy head. "Take the kids musseling? Get a sitter and drive over to the dunes?"

"You two decide," Max said, dumping Marlene off his lap as if he had forgotten how she came there in the first place. "I have work to do."

"*Work?*" Marlene said. "On such a beautiful day?"

Max gave her a pained look and walked out, saying over his shoulder, "Come up when you can, Shirley. I want to show you Part II."

"Excuse *me*," Marlene said, flopping down on the couch and stretching her arms high over her head. "Tell me," she asked lazily, "what does he do for amusement?"

"He likes movies," Mrs. Kane said.

"Movies?" Charlie said, coming in with a steaming cup of coffee in his hand. "Who's thinking of going to the movies on a day like this?"

"Nobody, silly." Marlene laughed. "We were talking about Max."

"I don't want to hear a word against him," Charlie said. "He may have a way of taking life too seriously, but he's really a grand guy at heart. Here's your coffee, Shirley. I was keeping it hot for you."

"Why, thank you, Charlie," Mrs. Kane said, lighting up.

"How about you, darling?" Charlie said. "Another cup?"

"I'd love one."

"Another cup?" Mrs. Kane said.

"Charlie brought me breakfast in bed this morning, didn't you, darling?" Marlene explained from the couch, raising her cheek to be kissed.

Charlie bent over and kissed it. Did he mean it, or was it an empty gesture? He meant it. Oh, well, she had never intended to be a home wrecker anyway. Mrs. Kane shrugged and walked over to the window where she could see the children playing outside. Betsy Krebs was sitting under a tree reading a book upside down. The others, her Sally and little Billy Krebs, were pouring sand over each other's heads while the dog raced around them, yelping. Mrs. Kane felt for the sneaker she had shoved into the pocket of her shorts. In a moment she would have to go out and trap Sally again, and when this was accomplished force herself back into the kitchen where the breakfast dishes waited for her in the sink—it was her turn today. Then, after that, there was always Part II upstairs. She sighed. Reality sometimes had a nasty way of taking over, especially in the morning. She wondered if she had not gone off on a wrong turning the night before, after all. Perhaps she was still meant for the life of art. Painting, for instance. All the other wives painted, so why not her? Apparently it was very simple. All you needed was a few tools and the desire to be creative. Seeing the stump of a crayon and a torn paper napkin which one of the children had left on the windowsill, she seized them eagerly. She worked for a few moments and then picked up the napkin and looked at it with a faintly puzzled air. It read:

2 doz. eggs

3 milks

1 can pineapple—*crushed*

By all laws of nature it was impossible that Marlene Krebs's hair should stay put in a fast-moving car with all the windows open. But there it was. Absolutely impeccable, just as it had been on the beach, in the bay, even in the sailboat that time when the salt spray had been dripping down Shirley Kane's own nose—Marlene had taken lots of pictures of that day. They were not developed yet. Perhaps there was still time to steal them from the general store and burn them. No, what was the point? Charlie Krebs had seen her with his own eyes, soaking wet, and it had not seemed to disturb him. Anyhow, why try to change at her age? Some people went through life cool and composed and others bravely bared their chests to experience. She liked that metaphor, though baring her chest did seem a touch too literal at the moment. Still, the day had been salvaged after all. The sitter who had promised to come that afternoon had really come that afternoon, and here they were off for a trip to the dunes. No children, no dog, and two whole hours to themselves.

"It's a bee-you-tiful day!" Mrs. Krebs sang out from the back seat.

Charlie Krebs, who was driving, caught her eye in the rear-view mirror and winked.

"A beautiful day," she repeated and winked back. Beside her Max remained glumly silent. Naturally, Max detested outings. He also detested lying in the sun, leisure, pointless conversations, and in the last analysis most people—with the exception of his Shirley and an elderly lady historian who lived in New York. Often, the very presence of other people offended Max, he could not see them as anything but deliberate time wasters with only himself left to hoe the hard row. By this Max did not mean physical labor. Good god, no—otherwise would he look like that in shorts? No, what Max saw himself as leading was a life of absolute unyielding thought, or as Max himself put it, a concern with—and here the *I* practically leaped out of his mouth and capitalized itself before her—*Ideas*. Until Max, she had never met anyone concerned solely with Ideas with a capital *I* and at first the picture of them marching sternly and resolutely across Max's brain, and presumably into her own, had absolutely enchanted her. By the time the enchantment wore off, after some three years or so, it was too late to back out. All the Ideas were already set up around her like little pickets in a fence. Sometimes of course she would still find herself making unthinking suggestions, like, "Max, let's go someplace on Sunday." But at this, Max would fix her with such an incredulous horrified stare and say, "You mean you have nothing *better* to do?" that she would always apologize immediately, "I'm sorry, Max, I wasn't thinking." (Though more and more lately it had been hard to figure out on the spur of the moment what *was* better than going someplace on Sunday.) How she had ever gotten him to agree to share a house for a month with the Krebs family she would never know. Of course, it was true what she had said that morning, that Charlie Krebs was Max's own discovery, a chance acquaintance grown to friendship after they had stood on a traffic island in the middle of Main Street for a half hour discussing Pushkin. And then Max did admire Marlene Krebs for her reserve, though cautioning his wife not to model herself after her. "You'll never make it, Shirley. Marlene was born in Boston, remember." Nevertheless, the original plan to share a house, tossed out by Charlie Krebs in a careless moment, had thrown Max into the doldrums. "Share a house? Share a house?" he had demanded emerging from his solitude like a bear from a cave. "Why?"

"Because we couldn't afford to take a house on the Cape by ourselves."

"That's not the point. What are you trying to escape from, surrounding yourself with all these people?"

"Oh, it's not for me, Max, dear, it's for the baby. Only child. So alone all day long." Gabble gabble.

At this Max had nodded thoughtfully. Yes, it was probably the picture of the baby surrounded by little playmates that had won him, that and the promise that if the three Kanes shared a bedroom there would be one left over for Max's study. And Charlie Krebs, where would he work? Well, as far as she knew, Charlie was going to take a vacation. And with that, Charlie Krebs had sunk all the way down the well of Max's estimation.

But now she was relieved and grateful that Max had only lent himself to this vacation and to this outing in particular, ready to take himself out at any moment. It meant that technically he was not really there and that with the exception of a pat or two and a little bone thrown to the Ideas once in a while she was as footloose and fancy free as a bird.

"Oh, the sea! How I love the sea!" she called out as the car stumbled and lurched to the small flat parking area at the top of the dunes. She crawled out of the car—why didn't somebody invent a way to get out of a car gracefully?—and the wind whipped the single braid up off her shoulder and spun it around behind her. "*Look* at it, *look* at it all spread out there. Inland is horrible. I hate inland. How can anyone *bear* not to live near the *ocean*?"

"It's the bay," Max said.

"Now, now," Marlene said in her gently chiding voice. "No need to be so intellectual."

To Shirley Kane's amazement her husband smiled. Now if *she* had said that—suppose Max were falling in love with Marlene. What a marvelous idea. Suddenly the world seemed full of delightfully unexplored possibilities. She felt a joyous kinship with her three companions as she skipped down the wooden stairs to the beach itself. There was no one else around except for two bald men spreading suntan oil on their white chests. Turning their backs on the aging bathers, the four of them promenaded on, bouncing and jouncing on the bumpy pebbles. It was low tide and the flat wet sand lay gray and glistening as the water lapped at its edges. Sandpipers minced their way in little straight lines. The sun slid out and in again behind a cloud, and the wind whipped at their skins. On and on the beach stretched, winding itself into infinity, and Mrs. Kane thought: *The world was all before them where to choose their place of rest.* Actually, the place they chose was near a little hollow in the dunes, not too far after all from the parking lot. The women stretched out their towels, tugged at the straps of their bathing suits and lay down on their stomachs. Then, because the flying sand stung their faces, they turned over on their backs, smoothing their thighs with outstretched palms. After a short appraising glance, Charlie and Max went down on the sand beside them resting on their elbows.

"How divine," Shirley Kane murmured, squinting at the skimming clouds.

"Utterly utterly," Marlene Krebs agreed.

"There's a passage from *Moby Dick* that says it all," Max offered. "Let me see if I can remember the whole thing." The others paused and gave him smiles of uneasy encouragement. Max failed to remember. They all sighed. Yes, it was marvelous, just lolling around on the beach, there was nothing like it. But they were not quite sure what to do about it. They could just lie there, of course, or else they all had books—two Graham Greenes, a Raymond Chandler, a complete Whitman—they could read them, or else. . . .

"How about a walk?" Max said enthusiastically.

No one answered. "Shirley?"

"Not now, dear. Later maybe."

"What about you, Charlie?"

Mrs. Kane looked up sharply.

"Hell," Charlie said, "we just got here. Why not wait a while?"

Mrs. Kane's mind clicked away like a giant computer. Two down and one to go. If only that one *would* go. But Max sighed, shrugged, and gazed listlessly out to sea. Go on, Max, ask her. Oh, if only she had some strange psychic power, if only she could beam a thought straight into his head. The thought zoomed against his skull and stunned itself senseless.

"Why not go alone, dear?" Mrs. Kane said, trying to unstrangle her voice. "Or better still—" she wet her lips and tried again, "or better still, why not ask Marlene? I bet Marlene would love to go with you."

"Marlene?" Max repeated blankly. My god, had he forgotten who Marlene was? "Oh, *Marlene*. Sure. How about it, Marlene, want to take a walk?"

Marlene raised herself on one elbow, and for one terrifying moment looked absolutely inscrutable. Mrs. Kane closed her eyes. "Why, yes," she heard Marlene say, "I'd love to." A long sigh eased its way out of Mrs. Kane's soul.

When she had collected herself sufficiently to open her eyes again, Max and Marlene were already tiny things mincing along and getting smaller. Low visibility. How wonderful. She turned her head gently to the other side. Charlie Krebs was looking at her. She reached out her hand and he squeezed her fingers. "Hi," he said.

"Hi."

"You don't like to walk, do you?"

"You asked me that yesterday, Charlie."

"Well, do you?"

"*Sometimes.*"

Charlie dropped her hand abruptly. Her heart gave a sickening lurch until she realized he was only rubbing his nose. "Goddamn this sand," he said. "It really stings. Come on. Let's catch up with them."

Catch up with them? Oh, Charlie Krebs, how can you suggest such a thing?

"You can go on if you want to," she said coolly, "but I'll stay here." Out of the corner of her eye she observed triumphantly that Charlie Krebs showed no signs of budging. But the windswept sand kept scratching at their faces until even she could no longer ignore it. Mrs. Kane looked around quickly and then—wonder of wonders—saw the hollow in the dune behind her, secluded, quiet, with its own little patch of crab grass, and—was this possible?—invisible from the beach.

"I know," she said. "Up there. I bet there's no wind in that hollow." Charlie squinted up dubiously. "Why don't I go first and try it?"

Horribly aware that this was not how she had planned it, Mrs. Kane scrambled up the slope of the dune practically on all fours. Then, reaching the hollow at last, she sat down cross-legged like an elf who sewed shoes. Charlie Krebs, on his feet now and looking more lean and long than ever, was watching her closely. If he asks me how it is, she told herself, I'll just tell him matter of factly that the wind's worse up here than down there. Then I'll come back down again and it will all be over. But if he follows me up here without asking, why then, why then. . . . Her heart began to pound and the suspense was unendurable. She stood up and turned her back on Charlie Krebs. Once more the world was all before her. Another hillock of sand, and then a hollow and then another hill, as far as she could see. The wind whipped at her body and struggled with the scrub pines, making her feel like a giant perched on a range of tiny mountains. Suddenly she felt Charlie's hands strong and demanding on her bare shoulders. She wheeled about madly, passionately, ready to throw herself into his arms, and knocked him down. For one hideous second she watched him flailing his arms and legs like an overturned turtle. Then she closed her eyes. Ha, ha, ha, said the nasty voice that sometimes spoke to her. Good try, but no cigar. Well, *sic transit gloria mundi*. But no, Charlie Krebs was back on his feet and asking for more! "Shirley, Shirley," he whispered.

"Charlie," she answered back. Then they were tangled up in each other's arms. Charlie Krebs went down again, on purpose this time, pulling her on top of him. The sand, the sea, the sky went swirling about. At last, at last, at last! Oh, Charlie is my darling, Charlie is my love. His hand moved gently but so knowingly up and down her thigh, across her back, around and under her throat.

Suddenly: "No, no, no, we mustn't."

But oddly enough it was Charlie Krebs speaking, not her.

"No, no, we *mustn't*," she repeated hastily, trying to make up in emphasis what she had lost in time. Having done her duty, she put her head back again on Charlie's shoulder and snuggled closer, until, catching the hint, she rolled off him onto her side.

"We've got to cut it out," Charlie whispered fiercely. "We're not kids anymore."

"Cut it out?" she said. "Oh, yes, of course. You're perfectly right." Secretly, however, she was puzzled. Why insist on their ages? They were hardly ancient or infirm—the evidence was marvelously fresh on this point. And besides, did *kids* go around doing this kind of thing? Why if she ever caught little Sally—but there was no time to think. His arm was tightening around her and his face was on top of hers. "We mustn't, we mustn't, we mustn't," they murmured deliciously, and then the swirling and swooning started all over again. Her mind swept clear away, leaving the rest of her on fire.

This time, however, she remembered the words in time. "Please, Charlie, please," she whispered. "Not here." Pushing him away weakly, she rose unsteadily to her feet.

Charlie caught her by the shoulder. "Hey, are you all right?"

"Of course I am."

"For a moment there I thought—look, Shirley, I'm sorry."

"What are you sorry about?"

"A man ought to have more control."

She glanced at him with surprise. To her his control was amazing.

"Maybe it's the way you're wearing your hair today," Charlie said, smiling. "It's sexy as hell, you know."

"Is it?" she murmured.

Charlie shook his fist at her and, lifting her chin, kissed her with a sureness that made her giddy. Then, catching hands as children do, they started to gallop down the steep dune. Out on the open beach they looked around simultaneously and seeing no one put their arms around each other's waists. Linked together they walked to the water's edge, planting their feet in perfect harmony. When she walked with Max she was always stumbling and lurching behind. But Charlie was different. He stooped a little to be nearer her height and took small steps to match hers. Charlie was wonderful. With Charlie she was a very model of grace.

"I'm glad you only come up to my shoulder," Charlie said, as they stood squeezing their toes in the lapping water. "I've always liked little girls."

She swallowed her sip of joy. Then silence. Then Charlie again. "Look, about before. I'm not sure what I ought to say to you," he said. "I think maybe I ought to explain—"

"Charlie, darling," she said urgently, "are you always so moral, or is it just me?"

"Well, I just didn't want you to—all right, never mind," Charlie said. "You're very cute." He looked around. "I wonder where they are," he said.

"Oh don't worry about them," she answered airily. "I'm sure they're having a fine time." But this was the wrong thing to say. Charlie's face stiffened. "I mean maybe they wandered off into the dunes too." Another wrong thing. Charlie's face got stiffer. Now, really, Charlie, you can hardly expect to have your cake and eat it too. Very deliberately, she rubbed her ear on Charlie's bare shoulder once or twice. Charlie went lax. There, it was all right now. It was perfect. Entwined together at the edge of the water. She could stand there for the rest of her life. Lap, lap, lap, went the ocean—no, the bay—filling up her cup of contentment. We have a secret, she thought, a beautiful secret. That she had no idea what this secret was only made it lovelier. Her cup of contentment brimmed over.

When she saw them coming she did not panic. Instead, with perfect aplomb, she withdrew her arm from Charlie's waist and nudged him gently with her elbow. Charlie got it. "Hello! Hello!" they cried, waving with perhaps a little more abandon than necessary.

Max and Marlene looked very pleased with themselves. "We had a great walk," Max said sternly. "You should have come too."

"Oh, we did walk," Mrs. Kane said blithely. "We just came back. Funny we didn't run into you."

"Were you in the dunes too?" Marlene laughed. "Down where we were we tripped over about ten couples necking madly."

Steady now, Mrs. Kane told Charlie. Hold on. Don't bolt until we hear the rest of it.

"Anyone we know?" Mrs. Kane asked pleasantly, leaping off into the icy brink.

"I don't know. We didn't stay long enough to find out. Not that *they* would have cared."

"Imagine that," Mrs. Kane remarked.

Charlie looked quickly up at the sky. "Does anybody," he said, "happen to have the time?"

Max did, naturally. It was time to be off. They picked up their books and towels, and started for the car. Charlie and Marlene walked on ahead, like an old married couple. Both of them were very tall—how's the air up there?—and she was left behind in the short world of her and Max. But for once in her life, Mrs. Kane didn't mind having shrunk. After all, hadn't Charlie himself told her he liked little girls? She looked idly at the back of the man who was walking with Marlene, feeling no connection with him and thinking instead of her own Charlie, the one she had left safely tucked away in the dunes. Later on, she thought with a sudden delicious wriggle, she might pay him another little visit in her mind, go through the whole thing step by step from that first extraordinary kiss until that—a lascivious grin flitted across her face.

And then Max, dearest darling beloved Max said, as he got in behind the wheel to take his turn driving back, that he would like to go to the movies that night.

"The movies? Good god, no," Mrs. Kane blurted out, right before the full luminousness of it dawned on her.

"What about you, Charlie?"

"Me? No, I don't think so."

"Marlene?"

For the tenth time that day, Mrs. Kane stopped breathing.

"Oh, I don't know," Marlene said finally. "Well, maybe. Oh, sure, why not?"

Was it true? Could fate really move so swiftly? Wouldn't Marlene suddenly turn capricious and change her mind? But no, they were already talking about times and last showings. So she and Charlie would really be alone that night. Humbled in spirit, reverent, a penitent whose prayer had just been answered, Mrs. Kane swore that after tonight she would never ask anything more again. Just to think that in five hours from now—she glanced at Max's watch—yes, say five hours to be on the safe side, she and Charlie would. She and Charlie. But no, they mustn't. We mustn't, we mustn't, we mustn't, Charlie's voice sang sweetly in her ear. He was really very protective, the angel. So gallant. Everything a man should be. By the sea, by the sea, by the beautiful sea, her heart sang as she slumped down in the seat beside Max, who had just released the emergency brake, and her feet beat out a tattoo on the windshield.

The blow came after dinner, when the last burbling child had been menaced into bed, this time little Billy Krebs, and the pots scoured, and the decision taken about whether the half a can of sardines would keep another day—it was pitched into the garbage can.

"You want to go to the movies?" Max said, as Mrs. Kane ambled into the living room with a stiff drink in her hand.

"*Me?*" she asked in horrified astonishment. "I thought you were going with Marlene."

"She doesn't want to see the picture."

"Why, what's playing?"

"*I Was a Teenage Werewolf.*"

"Oh." It came out like a little moan from her heart. She sank down in the big wing chair, staring at the ironically merry fire. So *this* was fate, the hand of God reaching out to protect her honor. Why couldn't He get busy on more important things? Look at all the floods or the earthquakes in Japan, to say nothing of wars and pestilence and disease. Like a pinioned fly, she fluttered up in one last struggle.

"Why not go anyway?" she said, craning her head sideways and addressing Marlene, who had draped her slender impeccable body on the couch. "I'm sure symbolically it could be very entertaining. I mean if you look at it one way, *all* teenagers are werewolves."

"Oh, don't go to the movies," Charlie Krebs said, coming in puffing his pipe. He lifted his wife's legs, sat down on the end of the couch, and put the legs back in his lap. "Why don't we all stay home tonight and read poetry?"

"What a wonderful idea," Max said, going off to find all his Oxford books of verse.

Poetry, Mrs. Kane thought grimly, taking a healthy swig of her drink. Poetry! Goddamn you, Charlie Krebs. Goddamn your cowardly uxorious lecherous aesthetic hide.

A round of drinks, another stiff one for Mrs. Kane, a moment for clearing throats, cracking book spines, scanning indexes, and blowing noses, and the poetry reading swung into motion—right over Mrs. Kane's dead body.

Both Charlie and Max loved to read aloud and privately they were much impressed with the resonance of their own voices. They roared out triumphant passages, sank into whispers for the darker lines, made little spitting noises for final *t*'s, acquired progressively more English accents, and soon in a perfect ecstasy of self-satisfaction were skipping happily from poem to poem as if they were so many stones in a rippling brook. From Shakespeare to Auden to Yeats to Thomas to Keats to Eliot they hopped, and if they occasionally fell into the water—"Are you *sure* it's pronounced that way?" or "Well, how did *I* know it ran to eight pages?"—they were quickly out again with a little shake and another leap. As the evening wore on, Mrs. Kane sank deeper and deeper into the dark regions of her soul. She thought of an essay by E. M. Forster on not listening to music, and seizing a line and twisting it out of shape, told herself that every time she listened to poetry all she could think of was how poetic she was. But even this was not true, she realized darkly—there darkly! Wasn't that a poetic word? The fact was that many people had read aloud to her, sweethearts, professors, Max had even attempted the whole of *Anna Karenina* every Tuesday night while she ironed, and each time no sooner was the first line spoken than the latch of her mind eased open and she wafted off into some private sphere of her own. What was the matter with her? Why did she fail so abysmally to connect with the recited word? Was her hold on reality so tenuous? On the other hand, god knew that what she had contemplated doing with Charlie Krebs tonight had a greater reality than listening to him read a bunch of poems, no matter what any critic said. She sniffed into her Kleenex. Her second drink had already transmogrified into a third, and her third into a fourth. With this last translation, a tiny hope sputtered up in her breast. She was a fool not to have been paying attention. Perhaps Charlie Krebs had not simply been choosing poems at random, but was reading each one to her, a message thrown by a lover over her garden wall. She decided to test this theory on Max, who for all she knew had been trying to send her messages too, and listened carefully as he read first, "Out of the Cradle Endlessly Rocking," and next—they were dividing them up two by two now—something by a bishop about his dead wife. Well, why not? Maybe he wanted another baby and at the same time he was afraid having it would kill her, which it would. She put her glass down carefully and closed her eyes for Charlie's turn. With the first rendition, selections from "Ash Wednesday," her heart sank. With the second, the tiny hope went out with a hissing sound. It was from Robert Frost to his little horse. She drained off what was left of her drink, swallowing the splinter of an ice cube. Forget him, forget him, forget him, she told herself woozily, this guy would rather listen to the sound of his own voice any day than make love to you. She wiped her eyes surreptitiously with her shredded Kleenex. Darkly, darkly, darkly, she repeated to herself, a very poetic word.

Had she been dozing? Marlene was now rising languidly from her couch and bidding everyone good night. But before hope had time to leap unbidden into Mrs. Kane's breast, Charlie was up too, and encircling his wife's waist with his arm. Sleepily, and with not an inch of space between them, they ambled away to bed.

"Good night, sleep well," Max said cheerfully. He stretched and yawned and scratched his ear with exhausted contentment. "They're really not bad people," he said. "Though I'm not so sure about her. A decided philistine streak there. But Charlie, on the other hand, well it's rare these days to find people who really care about poetry, who want to understand life in terms of it. You know, aside from you and Charlie, I can hardly think of any. With the exception of a few Europeans, of course."

"Of course," Mrs. Kane said.

Max leafed through the anthology on his lap with a little smile, reluctant to lay it down. "How about it?" he said. "Just one more? What do you want to hear?"

"'Dover Beach,'" his wife said bitterly.

"The sea is calm tonight," Max began. "The tide is full. . . . Ah, love, let us be true to one another," he concluded:

> "for the world, which seems to lie before us like a land of
>   dreams,
> So various, so beautiful, so new,
> Hath really neither joy, nor love, nor light,
> Nor certitude, nor peace, nor help for pain;
> And we are here as on a darkling plain
> Swept with confused alarms of struggle and flight,
> Where ignorant armies clash by night."

He closed the book slowly and looked at her. It was *that* look. Oh, no! Leaping up from her chair, she bade him a hasty good night and stumbled off to the bathroom. Maybe he would catch up with her later, maybe not. She had been speaking to him a great deal lately about the personal freedom of each individual and there was a chance some of it had sunk through. She took a long time washing her face, though away from the fire the bathroom was very cold. It was an old house full of chinks and spaces for the wind to come through. It was also, she realized, a very noisy house. All that creaking and groaning. Her hand, reaching for a toothbrush, arrested itself in mid-air. She raised her eyes slowly toward the ceiling. Billy Krebs. Billy Krebs waking suddenly and jumping up and down on his bed. Undoubtedly. Lowering her eyes again she caught sight of her stricken image in the bathroom mirror.

Several days later, looking back, Mrs. Kane could see very little to add to the credit side. A short wade out to the rushes with Charlie while

Max and Marlene and the babies watched closely from shore, and squeezing hands in the mud where the mussels lay. They had emerged at last with one hundred and twenty-five mussels. Then a quick kiss that day she was washing the broiler, and a drafty chilly embrace behind the open door of the refrigerator. Otherwise, nothing. And only one week until they all went back to Gorham.

And Max and Marlene, where were they in all this? It was hard to say. Marlene of course was as inscrutable as ever and each day Mrs. Kane distinguished in her so many different motives—approval, disapproval, indulgence, disdain, ignorance, omniscience, readiness to pounce, absolute indifference—that it always struck her with horror that perhaps Marlene had no motive at all. Max's nose, on the other hand, was quite clearly out of joint, though even here the motive was ambiguous, ambiguous that is for Max, who loved nothing better than to talk things over and get to the bottom of them. "Come outside, Shirley," he was whispering several times a day by now, "I want to talk to you," and each time she escaped by a hair. Once he had actually caught her for a moment while she was on her way to the general store with Sally.

"Where are you, Shirley?" Max had demanded point-blank, putting his face close to hers.

"Right here, of course," she had answered, backing away a step while Sally pulled at the skirt of her bathing suit.

"No, you're not. You're far away. In fact, I know just what you're thinking."

"Oh, really? Cut it out, Sally."

"You're thinking about sex," Max said grimly. "I can tell by the way you move your ass."

Tucking in her posterior daintily she sniffed and moved on. But as she bundled the baby into the car, she realized from the way her heart pounded what a scare he had given her. Not that she thought that Max was necessarily worried because it was sex that was on her mind. He would worry just as much if he thought there was anything on her mind she was not telling him about. Or what bothered him might simply be that she was with other people more than him. Max hated to see her actively involved with other people. It gave him the feeling that life was flowing on around him unchanneled and that he just had to get his finger in the dike. But if things were already so apparent to Max they might be to Marlene too. It occurred to her that she was really much more worried about Marlene than Max. It was one thing to toy with the idea of betraying your husband—wasn't there some unwritten law about no jury convicting you?—and another thing entirely to betray the person you had talked about your husband to. She thought about all those nice boozy conversations she and Marlene had had all winter long about how Max was unconsciously seeking to devour Shirley and how Shirley would probably liberate herself at last by sleeping with someone else. Oddly, these conversations still went on because Marlene, now that she was living in the same house with Max, was really warming up to her subject.

"You were so right about him," Marlene had said only that morning while the two of them sat on the beach watching the children climb in and out of an old abandoned rowboat. "He has the most voracious psyche I've ever encountered. I think he'd like to eat us all if we gave him a chance. Ugh," she added with a fastidious little shudder, "such intensity."

"Would you mind handing me the suntan oil?" Mrs. Kane said peevishly. She uncapped the bottle and rubbed the sandy oil on her nose. "I don't think," she said, "that intensity is quite the point. Max unintense would hardly be Max." But here she could not help sighing. "The only thing is, I wish he didn't have to be quite so intense about *me*."

"Exactly," Marlene said, spreading her towel behind her and lying back. "And that's why," she murmured, "I realize you're right to be thinking about having an affair with someone."

"You *do*?"

"Well, yes. I think that it will at least give you the illusion of freedom. You'll be having an intense but entirely private life of your own. And then, I think, you'll find you really love Max much more than you think you do now. You'll realize that you're living with him because you choose to, not because you've been forced into it."

"I will?" Mrs. Kane squinted down at Marlene suspiciously. And how do you know so much about it, Toots, she wondered, what have *you* been doing on the side? It was a question she had often longed to put to her. Was Marlene talking from specific experience or from simply a general and genial acquaintance with the facts of life? Someday Mrs. Kane would ask her point-blank: Look here, friend, she would say, have you or haven't you? But somehow the right moment never came up.

"Anyhow," Marlene was saying with a little yawn, "I should think it would be much better to do it and get it over with. Then it wouldn't be on your mind all the time. Though in your case"—another little yawn—"you'd probably be plagued with remorse."

"*Remorse?*" Mrs. Kane's spine stiffened. "And why should I in particular be plagued with remorse?"

"Well," Marlene said with a little laugh. "I think you're just that kind of person."

Again suspicion seeped out of Mrs. Kane's eyes. Just what was Marlene trying to put over on her anyhow? Was there some hidden warning in all this? But no, Marlene was smiling up at her affectionately. Marlene was probably her innocent and unsuspecting friend. And she herself? A heel, a worm, a viper. "Come on, Sally," she shouted, "get out of that rowboat. It's time for lunch."

And now here they were again, gathered around their fire in the chummiest possible way. Max asleep on the couch, Charlie squatting on his heels and poking at a smoldering log, and she and Marlene ensconced in the two big easy chairs each with a detective story in her lap. Another idyllic scene. Except that every time Max snored, Mrs. Kane was ready to get up and kill him with her bare hands. What had ever possessed her to marry such a man? she wondered. Had she been insane or desperately afraid she would die a spinster or what? She tried to remember the early days with Max, the pleasure of seeing him in a new dark flannel suit with a white shirt and a bow tie, and walking arm in arm across Washington Square, or holding hands over a small round table in a bar. But it was like chewing on an old piece of paper, joyless, juiceless, tasteless. All she could remember was the present Max, that bushy-browed chinless horror who had whined at them all during dinner. It was true, of course, as Charlie had suggested gently, that Max had had too many martinis beforehand. But too many martinis did not make the man. There was absolutely no excuse for Max's behavior, and she for one, she Shirley Ridgebolt Kane, would never forgive him. Never. Not if she lived another million years.

Max let out another snore, and at the sound of that short choked-up snort, Max's face at the dinner table once more rose up before her. She blushed with shame. "No, no, I won't keep quiet!" he had shouted, pounding his fists on the table, though they had long since ceased trying to shut him up. "I'll have my say, goddamn it, even if it isn't"—and at this point he had given a little sneer—"good manners. Good manners! What do they mean to me? *Truth* is the only thing that matters. And that's what I want to know. I want to know what the hell is going on around here. I have a *right* to know." Here his bloodshot eyes had wavered and his voice practically went out. "All the time whispering and laughing and telling secrets," he muttered, "the three of them. Private jokes, private discussions, private everything. Until a man feels he has no place to go in this world. But do I have a right to ask what's going on? Oh, no. *That's* not playing the game. *That's* not discreet. It's interfering with my wife's precious freedom that she's always talking about lately. Freedom! What the hell does she know about freedom, I'd like to know? She with her precious little fantasy life. Does she know freedom is what you fight and die for? Well, why doesn't anybody answer me? Or doesn't a husband have any rights around here?"

Mrs. Kane covered her face with her hands. It was all too horrible to contemplate. And the worst of it was the way Charlie and Marlene had soothed Max like a baby and ushered him to the couch. Then they had turned to her with pitying glances and said that Max would sleep it off. Well, she didn't care if Max slept for a hundred years and for her part they could have ushered him into the bay instead of onto the couch. Most of all, she did not want their pity. Max had ruined her life, that was all there was to it. He had exposed the ravages of her private life to the Krebses and now they would never feel anything but compassion for her. She thought of her old vision of dancing gaily into the surf with Charlie Krebs. Gone, exploded, smashed flat like a blown-up paper bag. Never again would Charlie see her as happy, self-contained, a carefree explorer in the delights of life. If Charlie ever kissed her now, it would be because her husband didn't understand her. Horrible. A fate worse than death. But never mind, sleep, Max, sleep. He had done his dirty work. He had snuffed out her love life and therefore the best part of herself. Tomorrow probably she would go off with little Sally and never be seen again. She could see the two of them marching resolutely into the sea.

Charlie Krebs got up off his haunches, having coaxed the fire into a blaze, and wiped his hands on the seat of his shorts.

"Anybody want to come for a row?" he asked. "The moon's out."

Mrs. Kane turned her head away. It pained her to look at Charlie, her poor shattered dream. It hurt to hear his voice.

"Max is asleep, poor thing," Marlene said. "And I'm almost up to the murderer. Why don't you take Shirley?"

There it was, pity again. Marlene sending her off with Charlie to cheer her up.

"How about it, Shirley? Just a short ride?"

She shrugged her shoulders listlessly. Well, why not. Better to go anywhere than stay here and listen to her husband snore. Without even bothering to say anything she got up and followed Charlie out the door. After they had walked a little way from the house, Charlie put his arm around her in the darkness, but she gave him a bitter little smile and shook his arm off. Better to make it clear now that she would manage all right by herself. Later on he might remember her courage, recall perhaps the utter poignancy of the way she squared her thin shoulders and set out to face her life alone. She walked on in silence hearing nothing from the night except a whippoorwill hooting monotonously and the little hiss and boom of the surf on the beach. Overhead a lovely moon mocked them with an even silver light. They cut across through the rushes to where the rowboat was tied, and water squished through the new sneakers she had bought only that morning. How ironic to think that a few hours before she had put them on together with her white skirt and only clean blouse expecting the most of the evening. Well, that was life. In an odd way it was comforting to know that she could never expect anything from it again. Charlie held the boat and she climbed in mutely, like a drugged slave letting herself be carried off. Then Charlie got in and took the oars. There was a sudden rock and splash on her side of the boat.

"Damn that dog," Charlie said. A pointy wet black head rose from the water and then a long paw laid itself, dripping, across her skirt. "Get down!" Charlie shouted. "Go home!" The dog whimpered at them affectionately.

"I think he's trying to be friendly," Mrs. Kane said.

"He's always trying to get into this boat," Charlie said. "He thinks he's a goddamn lapdog." Charlie bopped him gently with an oar and at last the dog slid away into the water. As Charlie rowed out into the bay, Mrs. Kane looked back at the pitiful little black head pointing at them hopelessly. She had heard that if you owned a dog long enough you began to resemble it. She wondered if you ever looked like a dog you only shared a house with. There was certainly some connection between her and that animal. Charlie rowed on, regular long steady strokes carrying them out. When Max took her out in a boat they went around in circles half of the time and she always had to be ready in the back to push them off the rocks. But Charlie as always was perfect in a boat, strong and manly and competent. The sight of him began to revive her, especially the wisp of smoke rising from the pipe clamped in his mouth and his large fine hands pulling the oars. His long legs brushed against hers. It was really a beautiful night, she suddenly realized.

"Well, Shirley?" Charlie said, shipping the oars for a moment.

"Well?"

He shook his head. "Shirley, Shirley," he said, "what am I going to do about you?"

"Do about me?" she said with a sad little smile. "Nothing at all. That's the beautiful part of it."

Charlie looked at her closely and started to row again. Was it possible, she wondered, that Charlie had not taken her out in the boat just because he was sorry for her? Could it be that for Charlie, Max and all, things were still the same as ever? She could hardly believe it. Yet there he sat with a curiously thoughtful look on his face that frightened her a little. A grassy bank rose up behind them. There was a bump and a lurch and the boat was still. Without a word, Charlie pulled her up and kissed her.

"Oh, *Charlie*," she whispered, resting limp with relief against his chest.

Charlie kissed her again, violently, and then gripped her by the shoulders and held her away from him.

"Damn it, Shirley," he said, "I can't keep my hands off you."

"I know, I know," she whispered, "me too."

"I don't know what's happening to me. I can't even think of anything else. Every night I sit around waiting for them to go to bed first. Every morning I wake up early hoping I'll see you. And then tonight— you don't know how I prayed no one else would get into this boat."

"Did you, darling, did you really? And all the time I thought—"

"You think too damn much," Charlie said. "You're always thinking." His arms tightened around her and suddenly, just as if she were dreaming it, she found herself lifted high in the air by Charlie's strong arms. In a moment she was lying on the grass with Charlie beside her. Then nothing else existed.

She struggled desperately to the surface. "No, don't, Charlie. I really can't."

Charlie took a deep breath and whistled it out. He lay back slowly. "Max?"

"Don't mention his name to me."

"Then what is it?"

"I don't know. I feel miserable all of a sudden."

"It's all right," Charlie said, comforting her in the darkness. "I don't want to force you into anything."

"You're not forcing me. Maybe it's just that we're all living in the same house—it makes everything seem so *unethical*. Maybe when we get back to Gorham—"

"How?"

She paused, looking up at the brilliant white stars. "I don't know."

"Look, Shirley," Charlie said. "I want to be honest with you. I've landed in this kind of thing before. Not the same way, but—hell, I promised Marlene. You know I love Marlene, don't you?"

"Yes."

"Then—god, I want you—what are we doing here anyway? Come on, let's go back."

"Do we have to?"

"Look, baby, I'm human."

"All right. Kiss me good-bye first." The grass rustled.

"By god, Shirley," Charlie whispered fiercely, "if we don't get out of here soon, I'm going to rape you right now."

Rape, rape. The most delicious word she had ever heard. Well, why not? Why resist it? She closed her eyes, hearing her heart roar like a waterfall. She thought of Charlie undressed, not how he would look but how he would feel. The long slithery feel of him. *Yes*, she said, *yes*. The hithering, slithering feel of him. *Night*.

And now he was licking her cheek. Surely an odd thing to do. But after all, what did she really know about love-making? Charlie was experienced. She stirred uneasily. Did he have to slurp over her eyelid? Really—

"Goddamn that dog!" Charlie said.

She sat bolt upright. "Where? What? Who?" she cried, blinking rapidly like someone suddenly awakened from a deep sleep.

"Right in your lap," Charlie said between clenched teeth. "The mutt must have followed us on shore."

She looked dumbly at the dog. In her dreams the dog had never come up and she was not quite sure how to proceed. The dog looked back at her with velvet loving eyes and began to lick her arm. Shrugging a little, she patted the dog's head. "What do we do, Charlie?" she said.

"Kill him," Charlie answered. "Go on! Go home!" After a short kick in the rump the dog scampered off into the scrub pines. They lay down again gingerly. In a moment the dog was back, hovering over them solicitously.

"Charlie, maybe he's somebody reincarnated."

"A first citizen of Gorham, probably. Go on you miserable cur, beat it!" The dog snuggled down between them and kissed them both fervently. Muttering a very dirty word, Charlie helped her to her feet. They clung together passionately while the dog licked at their ankles. "Okay," Charlie said. "I know when I've had it." He kissed her once more, a very gentle kiss on the side of the neck, and then they got into the boat and pushed off.

As they came into the open bay the dog floundered behind them, yelping piteously. Watching the animal, Mrs. Kane began to feel a curious attraction for it.

"Charlie," she said, "do you think we could—?"

Charlie laughed and stopped the boat. The dog came clambering over the side into her lap, soaking wet and shivering and dripping with clam mud. The clam mud stank. A beautiful stink, full of nature and fundamentals. Probably for the rest of her life whenever she smelled clam mud or even fish she would think of this night, and Charlie. She stroked the dog's gooey back with thoughtful tenderness. Suddenly it occurred to her that she was looking at the one living thing in the world who regarded her and Charlie as a couple.

"He *isn't* from Gorham," she said solemnly. "He *loves* us."

Charlie gave her an odd look and went on rowing.

"Ma-ma. Ma-ma. Peepee."

"Yes, darling, yes. In a minute."

Mrs. Kane rolled over and snuggled under the blankets. She was standing on a grassy hillock with Charlie, the two of them together in the night. Charlie kissed her. Then Charlie's strong arms lifted her high in the air, swept her off her feet like a hero in a movie. Up in the air so high. Like a diamond in the sky. Then he laid her down carefully. His precious jewel. Her heart went chute the chutes. Who could resist such strength, such masculine tenderness? *Why* resist?

"Ma-ma, pee-pee!"

"I told you darling, in a *minute*."

She was standing on a windy mountain with Charlie. Charlie literally swept her off her feet. He was murmuring madness in her ear.

"Ma-mah!"

She broke away from Charlie a moment and paused, wondering whether or not to include the dog. Better not. A lovely dog, she would adore him for the rest of her life, but even this dog had to know his place. Omit the dog. Now then, should she rejoin Charlie? No, she would leave him on the hill awaiting further delicious contemplation. Meanwhile, opening her eyes she saw that it was a ravishing day, a perfect sparkling morning. "I wake up early, hoping I'll see you," Charlie's last night's voice murmured in her ear. How sweet the world was. If God wanted her to die this minute, she would do it willingly, yield up her soul without a moment's hesitation. Only those who had never known perfect bliss were afraid of relinquishing life.

"Sweet Sally," she said, crushing her wriggling daughter to her bosom. "You will never know how your mother adores you."

Everyone was in wonderful shape. The children, chubby-faced and smiling, especially Sally who danced with glee when Mrs. Kane got up and took her to the bathroom; angel Charlie bustling over the coffeepot, his hair still shiny with the water from his comb; soignée Marlene whose enigmas had been left way down the road by now; and even Max. Max was contrite. Max had acted badly and wanted to be forgiven. He kept stretching out his hand tentatively like a mastiff begging for a handout. She accepted the paw with good grace. Max had made a perfect ass of himself to be sure, but with the new fullness of her heart she forgave him. After all, was it really ethical to blame your husband for spoiling an affair you were thinking of having with someone else? Never mind. There would be no affair. She was glad that Charlie had not succeeded in raping her last night. If they had slept together they would probably both be gloomy and tormented this very minute. As it was, she was as lighthearted and delirious as a bird. Charlie wanted her, she wanted him. Charlie thought of her first thing in the morning; she saw him go to bed every night with a pang. That was enough for her. She wanted nothing more than this shimmering suspension between them, and the chance sometimes to kiss him in the dark. Otherwise, no involvements, no entangling alliances. All she had dreamed about for her and Charlie she already had. The situation suited her perfectly.

It was Max himself—poor miserable Max, she really had him on the ropes—who suggested another excursion to the dunes that afternoon. Mrs. Kane agreed gracefully to the suggestion and even added that she was sure Charlie and Marlene would not mind waiting for the sitter while they went on ahead. That would give her and Max a little time to be together. Max gave her a look of mournful gratitude. When afternoon came, still humming to herself, she put Sally to bed for her nap, and then, leaving Charlie and Marlene dismembering crabs for that evening's dinner, set out with Max for the dunes.

In the car, Max was pitifully silent, a silence that gave her an odd but exceedingly agreeable sensation, especially when she realized that she had created it herself. How strong a happy independent woman could be, she thought, strong enough even to shut up a husband who normally never shut up, and this without being a nag or a shrew or threatening to divorce him. Naturally, she did not expect Max to stay shut up forever. He was simply for the moment a little frightened of and probably awed by the new Shirley Kane who had sprung up beside him. His poor child bride, his little weaver of fantasies—should she call him on that or not?—anyhow his wife, now a mature whole generous woman at last. It would take a little adjustment on his part to accept the new her, the person who no longer swayed in his wind; but she would patiently bring him along. He would resist in the beginning, of course, that was to be expected, but with the infinite capacity for gentleness which was now hers, she would give him the reassurance he needed and finally he would accept gratefully the fact of an integrated adult sharing his life.

"Hello, Max," she said tenderly.

"Anything I say," Max said, "will be wrong."

Quite right. Then why had he said it? Did this man have any idea how hard it was to be nice to him? Did he realize that she had come back from a glorious adventure of her own to be by his side? Really, when she thought of all the—she restrained herself in time. "Now, now, Max," she murmured, giving him a frigid little smile, "you mustn't be like that." They rode the rest of the way in silence, but she was no longer sure it was of her own making.

When they parked at the top of the dunes, she had a crazy idea for a moment that she was returning to the scene of the crime, but she quickly erased this thought from her mind. It was just that the beach was curiously pale and flat, not at all the windswept savage place that she remembered. Because it was earlier than the last time, there were still little clumps of bathers all along the water's edge, mothers grabbing the legs of crawling children while fathers dozed, suntanned adolescents eyeing each other's bikinis, piles of towels and pails and shovels and rubber rafts shaped like sausages. A very boring domestic scene. Où sont les dunes d'antan? Automatically she looked behind her to see if the Krebses' car was coming along yet. But it was still too early, and besides how could their arrival change anything? Of course, they *had* promised to bring a thermosful of martinis.

"Come on, dear," she said, linking her arm through Max's, "let's walk."

"Which way?"

"Oh, *Max*." With a faint sigh of exasperation she headed them off to the right and they marched along out of step as usual like two dangling links in a chain. Then, having accomplished nothing, they turned and started in the other direction, this time like an old couple taking a constitutional on shipboard.

"You know, Max dear," Mrs. Kane said at last, in her gentlest tone, "perhaps we really should have a little talk after all."

"What about?"

"Oh, for chrissakes, Max, if that's the attitude you're going to take—" Once more she recollected herself in time, and the icy smile which was by now second nature to her settled itself over her face. "Never mind, Max, dear," she concluded, "perhaps another time when you've collected yourself sufficiently."

"Oh my, oh my, ain't we hoity toity," Max said, in an exceedingly uncharming falsetto. He drew together his thick black eyebrows and scowled at a passing pair of sandpipers. "*She* wants to sleep with somebody else," he explained to them sullenly, "and *I'm* supposed to discuss it."

"That is not the case at all, Max Kane," his wife replied with perfect dignity, "and you know it."

"Oh yeah?"

"Yeah!" Mrs. Kane took a deep breath and composed herself again. "If you would stop addressing me like an adolescent reproaching his mother—"

"Leave my mother out of this."

"If you would stop addressing me in that manner, perhaps we could get somewhere. Now, as it happens, I have neither the desire *to* nor the intention *of* sleeping with anyone. I repeat: neither the desire nor the intention. However—and please pay attention, this is an important point—even if I did it would be totally irrelevant."

"*Irrelevant?*" Max cried. "*Irrelevant?* I suppose if *I* went off sleeping around it wouldn't bother you in the least. You'd never say a single word."

"Well, *did* I ever say anything about those MLA conventions?"

"Listen, nothing ever happened at those MLA conventions and you know it."

"Max, you are getting away from the point as usual," Mrs. Kane said. "I assure you I have no intention of reviving old grievances."

"Look," Max said, "if you want to leave me and go off with someone else just say so."

"I do not want to leave you. I want to live with you," Mrs. Kane said, enunciating each word carefully as if she were speaking to a subnormal child. "However, and this is the point I have been attempting to make, I do not want to live with you on the old, and if I may say so, tired basis. My feeling is that we have somehow—and I'm not interested in putting the blame on anyone—forced ourselves into an artificial and uneasy intimacy. We not only have to tell each other everything, we're not even supposed to *think* things we can't tell each other. As a result we are both under an unnecessary strain. Now I really don't believe this kind of thing is necessary to a happy married life. I've been watching the Krebses and they—"

"You've been watching the Krebses too damn much."

"—and they seem to lead a much more relaxed life. They allow each other latitude in the everyday stresses of living. I think this is possible for us too. I think that if each of us really felt entitled to a private life—and, yes, this goes for having an affair too—we would be able to see each other as independent fulfilled individuals. And the result would be not only that we would love each other as much, but even more deeply. Because our love would really have meaning. Now, what do you say, Max? Do you see what I mean? Can you get the beauty of it? You know, laissez-faire and all that?"

Max looked at her quietly for a long time. He shook his head in wonder. "It's a miracle," he said, "an absolute miracle, that you can stand there and talk such crap."

Fortunately, the Krebses' car rolled up soon after that, and their friends came out smiling and content, apparently the crab meat had come off easily, and waving the martini thermos. In a way, Mrs. Kane was much gladder to see the martinis than the Krebses. The scene with Max had not disappointed her exactly—Max was by now incapable of disappointing her, so little hope did she have of him—but it had left her feeling insipid and flat. It was awful to rehearse and rehearse and then deliver oneself, only to find that the audience had gone home. She wished Max actually would go home and while he was at it take the Krebses along with him. A little solitude would suit her fine now and also the chance with the help of that beautiful thermos to commune with herself for a while instead of with all this—she realized it for the first time—rather inferior company. But of course everyone stayed—what had any of them ever cared for her feelings?—and soon they were all lying in their old places under the hollow in the dunes, carefully measuring the martinis among them while the talk swam in all directions. Mrs. Kane lay back with her eyes half-closed, sighting a large sailing vessel on the horizon.

"A bunch of explorers are sailing up to discover us," she said. "What shall we tell them is the name of this place?"

"How about Cape Cod?" Marlene suggested.

"An obvious absurdity," Mrs. Kane said.

Charlie Krebs, leaning on his elbows and looking up at her, smiled. But for the first time the sight of him failed to bring her back to life. He had a rather foolish smile, now that she came to think of it. He appreciated her too readily. Surely this showed a lack of discrimination. The uneasy thought came to her that perhaps somehow Max had been in back of this whole business with Charlie Krebs all the time. A hideous idea. She banished it at once. The martinis were very strong. Everybody said so while they had another. Did that thermos really hold a full quart? Charlie Krebs assured her that it did while he ran a finger along her arm. She looked blearily at Charlie's finger and then at Marlene and Max. Marlene was smiling at her husband indulgently and Max was gazing off into the distance as if he were oblivious to them all. Actually, there was no need for him to take this high and mighty attitude, since if you looked at him closely he was extremely blurred and out of focus, and therefore drunk. So was Marlene for that matter. Charlie too. How had they managed to get potted so quickly?

A contemptible crew. Grown-up people ought to be able to hold their liquor better than that. Suddenly, she had an overwhelming desire to sleep, and closed her eyes.

When she opened them only a few seconds later, she announced that it was going to rain, the sky had gotten so dark. The three of them laughed stupidly.

"Iss getting late," Marlene explained politely. "Have to go home."

"I doan wanna go home," Mrs. Kane said.

"Have to," Marlene said. Her wavering glance suddenly fell on Max, and a foolish smile lit up her face. "I know," she said brightly. "You stay here with Charlie. Max'll take me home." She rubbed her cheek provocatively on his shoulder.

"Hmm?" she murmured.

"No, no, no," Mrs. Kane said. "Doan want *anybody* to go home." She wondered why they were all acting so peculiar, why Marlene the reserved had draped herself so wholeheartedly over Max, and why Charlie was smiling at her so amorously without any attempt at concealment. "Doan want *anybody* to go home," she insisted, shaking her head. But no one paid any attention except for a short laugh all around. She felt a sudden cold foreboding as she realized that all along she had wished Max and Marlene would vanish and they always stayed, while now. . . . In a moment Max and Marlene had staggered off, and she was left alone on the beach with Charlie, a Charlie moreover who was gazing at her with liquid brown almost bovine eyes that shone out from behind the glasses. She looked around in the gathering darkness. There was no one else on the beach. Not a soul. A chill panic seized her.

"Let's have a drink," she said to Charlie in a tiny croaking voice. Charlie nodded. He tipped the thermos into her paper cup and then his own, waiting patiently until the last laggard drops had run out. They drank. And all the while Charlie never took his eyes off her. She swallowed hard. The next thing she knew Charlie was pulling her into the hollow in the dunes overhead. He started to grapple with her, panting and calling her name. "Charlie, Charlie, Charlie," she whispered frantically, "listen. . . ." If only he would stop for a minute, let her catch her breath, figure out what she was doing here, restore her befuddled senses. If only she could have a minute to sober up in. Oh, god, how she wished she were sober. But there was no time at all, only the great rush of Charlie beside her. Suddenly Charlie held himself off from her, his body tense.

"Wait a minute," he said, breathing heavily. "Maybe they haven't gone yet. Let me run and take a look."

"What are you talking about?" she said. "You can't go now."

But Charlie was already loping down the dune. She stared after him with horrified amazement. What kind of a man had she fastened her dreams on? How could he desert her at such a moment? How could he think so cold-bloodedly about Max and Marlene? It was as if someone had just pointed a finger at her and told her she was on the verge of betraying her husband. She sat up and fumbled at her disheveled clothes with witless hands, feeling at once desolate and ridiculous. If only there were some way of escaping, of letting Charlie come back and find her gone. But it was hopeless. Miles and miles of empty sand surrounded her. Above, the sky was dark and heavy, turning rapidly into night.

Charlie came back and flung himself down beside her. "They're gone, they're gone," he panted, groping for her body. "Oh, *darling*."

End it now, she told herself. End it anyway at all and never mind the rest. "I'm sorry, Charlie," she said in a quiet deliberate voice, "but we don't seem to understand each other. When you ran off just now, I'm afraid you brought me back to reality."

But as she should have realized even before she spoke, she had ended nothing. Charlie merely nodded and smiled—so he was beyond even listening to her now—and took off his glasses. The gesture terrified her—she felt a sudden sickness in her stomach—and the face it revealed was that of an eager hungry stranger with exposed shiny eyes. "Charlie, Charlie, please," she gasped. "Please, please," but she no longer even knew what she was pleading with him for. It was too late. "Charlie, Charlie, *please. Oh.*" Much too late. And it was like—oh, god, how horrible to think this now—it was so much like being with Max. She gave a little moan and closed her eyes, weeping softly to herself.

After a while, Charlie's head stirred on her breast.

"Did you?" he whispered.

"Does it matter so much?"

"I wanted to give you pleasure."

Pleasure. A little pang of tenderness welled out of her heart and she touched Charlie's cheek with the tips of her fingers. "We'd better go home now," she said softly. "You go on ahead to the car. I'll meet you there in a minute."

She closed her eyes again and did not open them until she was sure Charlie had gone. Then she got up slowly, clutching forlornly at her gaping blouse. The night had locked her in for good now. In the thick blackness there was nothing but the sucking sound of the sea and far off the hazy lights of Charlie's car. She was utterly alone. She was absurd. She stood there in an agony of desolation. "Max! Max!" she shouted suddenly in the darkness. "Where are you, Max? I need you."

Charlie's lights flickered on and off, and gathering up her possessions, a kerchief, a sweater, a beach basket, she clutched them against her and went stumbling and lurching down the black sand, crying like a child all the while: "Max, Max, Max."

For the first time in his life Max did not ask any questions. When she came crying into his bed in the middle of the night, he took her in his arms, and loved her. She loved him back. It was far more than she deserved to have Max waiting for her at the end of such a journey, and she tried by holding onto him as tightly as she could to make up for the thick wall of remorse separating them. Remorse. How right Marlene had been. How right everyone had been. Except that even Marlene could not have guessed what a strange shape Shirley Kane's remorse would take. Quite unwillingly, she remembered the wild ride home with Charlie in a car swerving drunkenly from side to side in the thick yellow fog. She remembered crawling all over Charlie and smothering him with kisses. She remembered that two times Charlie had stopped by the side of the road and—she burrowed deeper into Max's shoulder. What a night. With any luck at all, she would never survive it. Her head ached, her stomach ached, every tooth in her mouth was enormous and dry. Could a new morning really come after such a night before?

But of course morning did come, absolutely audacious in its brilliance. The sun-swept sand outside her window was dazzling and the air was pierced by the screaming laughter of the children. She heard coffee cups rattling and muted voices at the breakfast table. How could she ever face this day, she wondered, painfully ungluing her sticky eyes and stumbling into the bathroom. She scrubbed her face clean and pulled her hair straight back with an old rubber band. Surely they had only to take one look at her and they would know. But to her amazement, everyone, even Charlie dishing out the coffee, wore a lunatic mask of sanity, and the morning went merrily on completely on its own momentum, offering her the usual eggy dishes to wash and the choice of sunsuits for Sally. It was more than she could bear.

"Angel, darling," she whispered to Max, drawing him aside after lunch, "what do you say we get out of here tomorrow instead of waiting for the end of the week? I'm as sunburned as I'm ever going to be and this place is getting to be *such* a bore."

Angel Max, darling Max agreed. It was okay by him, he said, adding wisely that he'd known she'd get tired of it sooner or later. She looked at his sweet serious face, wondering what had ever made her doubt even for a moment that she loved him. The rest of the day she spent looking for Sally's other sneaker in out-of-the-way places and washing clothes in the hidden recesses of the cellar. If she could only avoid Charlie for the next few hours, then it would be all over. Perhaps in time she would even come to believe that nothing had ever happened between them, or if it had—one had to face facts after all—that it hadn't really counted. Of course it didn't count. How could it count? She had been drunk as a coot. That night she retired early, hand in hand with Max, and slept almost though not quite the sleep of the just. In the morning she arose promptly and scurried around, throwing bundles of things into suitcases and helping Max carry them out.

At last they stood, the four of them, in the open clearing around the cars, saying good-bye and that they had had a wonderful time and that there really wasn't any need to say good-bye because they would be seeing each other in a few days back in Gorham anyway, while the three children and the dog played tag around their legs. Mrs. Kane congratulated herself silently. She had done it after all. They were all packed and ready to go, and in a few minutes she would never need to see Charlie again. Never see Charlie again? What was she saying? Suddenly the others blotted themselves out and only Charlie was standing before her, young and tall and radiantly handsome.

"*Charlie*," she said, as her mind worked furiously. "Charlie, could you please take me to the laundromat? I forgot some stuff there and I can't leave without it. No, Max, it's all right. You wait here with the baby." While Marlene and Max stared, she pushed Charlie into the car and made him drive off. She looked back. Max and Marlene had not yet recovered and there would be hell to pay later on, but it was worth it. How could she have ever thought of leaving Charlie without being alone with him just once more? Charlie turned off into a deserted dirt road and stopped the car.

"They're furious," she said. "I'm sorry. I just couldn't think of anything else."

"You're really something," Charlie said, turning around to look at her.

She smiled at him uneasily, wondering what was happening to her. Always she had thought of herself as a woman of iron will, a woman who made pacts with the dark powers of the universe and stood by them unflinchingly. Yet only the other night she had made a solemn vow never to see Charlie again and she had broken it already. It was to have been the price, and a tiny price, of getting out of all this unscathed. Now here she was, not only seeing Charlie again, but having snatched him right out from under the noses of his wife and her husband. And for what? she wondered. Was it simply to say good-bye to him in private?

"Good-bye, Charlie," she said.

"Good-bye."

"Is that all you're going to say to me?"

"What do you want me to say?"

"Nothing, I suppose." She looked past him through the window where the brown dirt road soaked up the sunlight. It was going to be a long hot ride back to Gorham.

"Charlie?"

"Yes?"

"Did the other night count?"

"It counted," Charlie said.

"Very much?"

"Not as much as it might have. We'd be great together, you know."

"I know."

A car went rushing by out on the main highway. The two of them stiffened into attitudes of furtive innocence, relaxing gradually as the last skidding sound died away.

"Come into the back seat," Charlie said.

"No." What was the use, since she was sure to make a mess of it? The first noise and she'd probably run down the road screaming, she who had gone around masquerading as a fearless child of nature. She sighed deeply and rested her head against Charlie's shoulder.

"Oh, how I wish we could find some private place," she said dreamily. "With a big bed and lots of sheets and a door that locks. I wish we could have lots and lots of time, at least enough to get undressed. Do you realize I've never seen you without clothes on?"

"Would you like to?"

"*Charlie*, leave your glasses on. I'm not talking about now." She swallowed hard. "And—and afterwards, we'd have a cigarette and a drink and we'd lie around talking. And then we'd fall asleep holding each other. And whenever one of us woke up he'd turn over and the other one would still be there." Her voice faltered as she turned to him. "Don't you see, I want to be *connected* with you."

Charlie took her in his arms and she clung to him until a new unexpected fear made her draw away.

"Suppose it was awful," she said. "Me, I mean. You could be horribly disappointed. You could be sorry you ever—"

"Stop it," Charlie said, kissing her in a way that made her shiver. For one last blissful time she settled back against him.

"Tell me about the other times, Charlie."

"No."

"I don't mean what you did. I mean how you arranged it."

Charlie looked down at her and smiled. "Well, of course there's always the back seat of the car."

"Oh."

"Or else—I don't know." He glanced away with a faint frown.

"There's your own house, I suppose. Or a friend lends you an apartment. Or you go to a hotel."

"In the middle of the afternoon?"

"If there's no other time."

She looked at him with respectful admiration. How strong men were. How completely they took things into their hands. She closed her eyes as the picture came into her mind of Charlie marching into her kitchen in Gorham to demand that she come away with him that very hour. She would protest, of course, tell him that she couldn't leave her husband and baby—to say nothing of her dinner on the stove. But Charlie would only laugh at her excuses. He would grab her by the wrist, force her into his car, and carry her far away, having made all the arrangements, to some little motel nestled in the mountains. The lovely vision faltered and fell away. Charlie make arrangements? That was the best joke yet. Poor Charlie, what had he ever done, except be willing? It was she who had dreamed the whole thing up single-handed, she who had planned and schemed and even—she blushed to think of it now—dragged him off bodily this morning. No, there was no use waiting for Charlie to make the next move. The next move was up to her, and knowing that she would never make it, she also knew that everything was over.

Charlie's face was still turned away from her, looking in sharp profile more boyish than she had ever seen it. His cheek was almost pathetically smooth from eye to chin and the faint frown barely creased his forehead. Even his straight nose with its flared nostrils seemed curiously vulnerable in its beauty. I'm the Red Queen, she thought, and he was only part of my dream. And also—how odd to understand this only now—she loved him.

"I love you, Charlie," she said.

"I love you too," Charlie said, "I thought you knew that."

She nodded, yes of course she had known, and pressed her forehead against the window. "I'm sorry about the back seat," she said.

"Don't be sorry, darling. There'll be other times for us."

"Other times?" she repeated. Away from the sun and the ocean, back in fat pompous Gorham? Never. To Charlie, she said, "Yes, of course there will," and in a way it was worse first loving Charlie and then lying to him, than when she had thought she was saying good-bye to him forever.

When they came back, Max was already sitting in the car waiting for her. She got in beside him with Sally on her lap, forgetting entirely to explain about the laundry. Marlene kissed Max good-bye through the open window and through the other side Charlie kissed her. As Charlie drew away, Mrs. Kane thought of the old philosopher who had looked up at the stars and promptly fallen into a well. It was the last thought that came to her before they backed out and started down the sandy road, with the dog and little Billy Krebs running along behind them.

How I Spent
My Summer Vacation

FOR THE FIRST WEEK OR SO there was hardly a cloud in the sky, and what with one thing and another they had all been squinting up at it a great deal. But no, the weather stayed fine, unusual on Cape Cod, and there was also the fun of pretending to be a typical American family: Mother, Father, Big Boy, Little Girl, Colored Maid, all rosy-cheeked and beaming, like the picture on the back of a box of cornflakes, which only Big Boy ate. Anyway, it was only a temporary tableau since it was hardly their style. In actual fact, the maid, more of a mother's helper, was due in Tuskegee in mid-August, and the month that Arthur's son, Jason, was supposed to stay with them according to the terms of the settlement had dwindled to the first two weeks in June because he was going to International School in Switzerland. (Other summers, on account of a rich mother, there had been sailing camp in Maine, a children's archaeological dig in Mexico.) At which point Arthur would return to work on his *Further Readings in Sociology*, and Janet to her novel. But meanwhile it was wonderful to realize again, after having secretly resented starting their vacation so early on account of Jason, who usually came to them at the end of the summer, and giving up so much privacy, also on account of Jason, who occupied space in a kind of geometric progression, seeming to count for four extra people to everybody else's one, and renting an expensive three-bedroom house, and importing the mother's helper all the way from the dusky under-side of the tracks in Gorham, all of it on account of Jason, that he was really an awfully nice boy. "You see, darling?" Janet said, calming an always-anxious Arthur as they made a hasty trip to the First National for still more fruit, Kool-Aid, and barbecued potato chips. "It's just like everything else. A little common sense, patience, above all intelligence, and a child of divorce is as easy to deal with as your own." "He is my own," Arthur reminded her at the cash register, looking suddenly very skinny and full of Adam's apple. She put her hand over his on the wire shopping cart to reassure him, and then they drove back, bucking deeper and deeper into the sandy woods to a house that was in itself also a reason for self-congratulation, their best rental in years, maybe because this time Janet had made Arthur drive up and take a look: modern, gray and boxy, set high on stilts at the edge of a large breezy lake, so that when they climbed up on deck with their grocery bags they were immediately at sea, windswept and fragrant. The children rushed out between the sliding glass doors, little Googie to give Janet a bone-crushing hug around the waist and a kiss that landed on the sober belly of her Bermuda shorts, Jason just to poke around, filching cookies and potato chips, until the maid, also wearing shorts, surprisingly conservative ones with a little rosebud pattern, rather like Janet's, discreetly appeared to remove the grocery bags out from under Jason's inquisitive nose. Later, joining dark immutable Doris in the kitchen area, Janet looked out through the window at mossy green moors cleft with silver and then over toward the living-room area where Arthur squatted by the open black wrought-iron fireplace, accepting rolled-up strips of newspaper and dribbly, twiggy kindling from the eager children, and thought of some of those awful faculty wives in Gorham like silly Shirley Kane, who ran around like a chicken with its head cut off, or for that matter Betty Carlsbad, women who had no thoughts beyond child-rearing and domesticity, and didn't want anybody else to have either, who thought they were doing something great swapping fake gourmet recipes out of Julia Child; and realized how easy it was to beat them at their own game. Not that she wished to beat them at it indefinitely, only, to be frank about it, during Jason's two weeks, after which it was back to the novel. But how interesting to know she could do it if she wanted to.

"No, I'll never be able to thank you enough," Arthur said, putting it somewhat negatively as usual, when they stole away one evening to walk for a few minutes along a rose and silver sea. "You're so wonderful with him."

"But I'm enjoying it all *immensely*," Janet said, half-smiling, half-extracting a piece of that evening's beef stroganoff (Julia Child, *op. cit.*) from somewhere between her back teeth. It really had been a lovely day, swimming, snorkeling at this practically deserted beach, anchoring their kite in the sky while they sat cross-legged peering into Janet's plastic Baggies with many *oh*'s and *ah*'s (she was making great strides at lunch too), returning home for the beef stroganoff at an hour, five thirty, when most people didn't dream of such things, settling down for a peaceful game of Go-Fish while the fire sap hissed in the grate and Doris finally got up to do the dishes.

"I'm sure he has a crush on you," Arthur said.

"Oh, Arthur," Janet said, laughing rather nervously, "I doubt that." Though it was funny that Arthur should bring it up, since only that afternoon Jason had crawled over to her beach towel, bunching it up with sand, and whispered that she could make a fortune endorsing leg makeup on TV. A silly, touching moment, especially to someone who, unlike Jason's mother, had never pretended to beauty or glamor, but she had thought it best not to mention it.

"And when I think of those bitter, bitter two years before I met you, when—"

"But darling, why dwell on old unhappiness? Anyway, I love Jason, I always have. He's a charming boy. Even now, at thirteen."

"Charming?" Arthur said, reflecting the pink of a sunset sky.

Afterwards, examining the situation from every conceivable angle, Janet could simply find no hint of what was to come a few days later. Far from it. She had slept late on that particular morning—why get up early?—run a quick neat brush over her hair, and sat at the kitchen counter drinking coffee and trying to teach Googie how to read the labels on the Finast grape jelly and Arthur's jar of wheat germ. She was also pondering the possibility of a dinner party when Jason left. Doris, the colored mother's helper, was out back hanging up the laundry in the cranberry bog, and Arthur was down below in the studio/ garage apologetically catching up on his mail. Where she would work, Janet wasn't sure, probably in the bedroom as usual, though again not before Jason left. Meanwhile, perhaps Arthur would like today's picnic on the bay for a change if the tides were right and if she could find the Cape Cod souvenir calendar with the tidal chart on the back of it. She wondered if it had possibly found its way into Arthur's studio, and as she descended the rickety outside stairs hand in hand with Googie to ask him, heard his voice speaking with some annoyance to Jason. Again not in itself unusual, since Jason had a way of insinuating his presence when even the word "work" was mentioned. Nevertheless, she gave the partially open door a couple of quick knocks before she widened it and stepped into the sudden cool garage-like darkness. The car itself, a new red Volvo that they had bought in time for the trip, was outside in the sandy driveway, but the long dim canoe that had come with the house and also its lacquered oars were still affixed to the wall behind Arthur's work table, with Arthur himself half-risen before it. Jason was looking at him urgently, like a student with a late paper. Their faces turned to her in mid-flight.

"Seven hours sleep a night," Jason said with tears in his voice. "And my stomach's upset all the time. I just can't take it."

"Whoops," Janet said, retreating a step or two backward, and yielding to Googie's tug of the hand to let her scamper away. "I seem to be interrupting. Forgive."

"No, stay," Arthur said, glaring at a very trapped Jason. "You'll be glad to hear he wants to go home."

"I didn't say I wanted to go home *tomorrow*," Jason said. "I said Friday. Which makes it ten days. So where's the big deal, ten days or two weeks? You and Janet want to work anyhow."

"Oh, well—" Janet began.

"Never mind about our working," Arthur said. "And there happens to be four days difference between ten days and two weeks. What the hell do you think this is, a jail sentence?"

"Seven hours sleep a night," Jason repeated, crying openly. "I can't live on it."

"Listen," Arthur said, taking a gentler and therefore more ferocious tack, "we love you. We took this large expensive house on account of you. And first you were going to stay a month, then it got down to three weeks, then two, and now you want to make it ten days. Don't you realize how much we've given up for you? My work, Janet's work—"

"Oh, well," Janet said.

"—we even started this vacation so goddamn early none of our friends are here yet. And still you have the nerve to. . . ."

Janet slipped away, heart pounding, and went to sit on the scratchy bottom step of the outside staircase where she could be found in case of need. But oh, how awful. How sickening, literally. She really felt quite sick to her stomach as when she had drunk too much at a faculty party. And there was the same roaring in her ears. Oh, how awful. To have been so betrayed, and by a boy of thirteen whom they had taken in and made one of themselves. Googie marched by in her little polka-dot sunsuit and she automatically grabbed her, sand pail and all, instinctively closing her ranks. And what must poor Arthur feel, Janet wondered, kissing the top of Googie's warm little head over and over and stroking it with a trembling hand, still in there, poor darling, making one psychological gaffe after another. For of course it had been utterly stupid to make Jason feel he had to repay them for sacrifices he had never asked for in the first place. What purpose could that ever serve except to place an additional and intolerable burden of guilt on the boy? Didn't Arthur remember his own child-hood? Not that she felt particularly sympathetic to Jason's burdens at the moment. Only why hadn't the idiotic child had the sense to come to *her* with his bellyache? How ridiculously easy it would have been to divert him with some more of those insanely expensive whiffle balls from the News Dealer, or still another unnecessary piece of snorkeling equipment, or a trip to the penny-arcade amusements of the wharf at Provincetown on the pretext of visiting Dr. Hefflinger. She looked down at Googie, who had wriggled and squirmed to get away and then come back immediately to plant a pair of sandy elbows on Janet's knees, and look up, backside raised and inquiring. Such a happy hot sweaty little face. But hadn't Jason been happy too? Could she have been *so* mistaken in thinking that he was? She thought of him on his first visit years before, getting off the little plane in Provincetown in a crooked baseball cap, grinning from ear to ear. And of holding him in the middle of a nightmare while he cried, "I'm weady! I'm weady for the pitch!" And of sweeter moments playing Go-Fish and dominoes and I-Doubt-It, and watching her sister's daughter, who was also visiting, carefully print out the alphabet for him on a piece of shirt cardboard, of discreetly asking Betty Carlsbad why he had begun to smell like a goat ("Glands," Betty said), of endless beach picnics, and heady whispered compliments about her legs, on a crumpled beach towel. But what if Jason hated beach picnics? What if he disliked all group activities? Could all her instincts, all her experiences have misled her so badly? Oh, how quickly the world could change, shatter, dissolve. It was like that Friday night so long ago when, no older than Jason herself, she had watched President Truman declare a national state of emergency about Korea on TV, too terrified to ask her parents what it actually meant. And of course the full historic implications did not dawn on her until much later.

Sooner than she had expected, Arthur and Jason filed out, one behind the other, Arthur dark brown and skinny in his new striped shorts and matching terry-cloth lined jacket, Jason plump and pink and bare to the waist, with a pair of tight-fitting yellow satin lastex bathing briefs beneath. For the first time Janet remarked that the boy had no ankles, and that his legs descended like childish pillars straight into his high-laced sneakers. The discovery was vaguely irritating. Oh, god, what a relief it would be to tell him he was free to go home anytime, and that . . . she stifled still another misleading impulse. But would her instincts always betray her, Janet wondered through a sudden stab of pain, would she never be able to trust them again? Because of course, the *worst* thing they could do would be to let Jason end the visit on his own say-so. She must point this out to Arthur the first chance she got. "No, Arthur, the point about having a father, being a son, is that it is *not* a voluntary association." Except that for the rest of the day there was no chance to explain anything to anybody since, oddly enough, and this was even more disconcerting than the ankles,

Jason's attitude toward *her* didn't seem to have changed at all. If anything, he was even friendlier. "Hi, Jan," Jason said, draping a heavy bare arm on her shoulder buddy-buddy style, and later on all through the pebbly picnic at the bayside, which she had wanted not to suggest after all, but couldn't think *why* not, kept throwing himself down affectionately beside her, kicking up sand on poor Arthur, whose dark bony face lay at their feet, eyes squeezed shut against a painful sun. Was it possible, Janet wondered, watching Jason anoint himself with her suntan cream, first dribbling then smearing, or run waddling into the bay with a frogman's equipment to reappear a few moments later as a curved tube balancing a ping-pong ball and a yellow satin behind bobbing up and down in the endlessly rippling blue water, was it possible he didn't realize she was Arthur's ally, not his, and if she ever divorced his father she would probably never even see him again? The point was so crystal clear, as was the tone of voice in which she would make it, that she hardly paused to wonder why she was thinking of divorcing Arthur at all.

The maid, looking like night against a desert sky, helped Googie build a sand castle, which collapsed, and they all started home. "Right on, darling," Janet whispered facetiously to Arthur, who had nodded gloomily in advance, and then waited tensely to keep him calm when Jason made another scene about going home, dropped the other shoe on them as it were. But no, Jason remained strangely relaxed and cheerful, like a student radical who had left behind a time bomb and then happily telephoned about the explosion. "I want to go *home!*" Googie suddenly cried in her Mickey Mouse voice at dinner, working through some private grapevine of her own, and Janet glanced sharply across the table. But still Jason merely laughed. "Be *quiet*, Googie," Janet said, and reminded her what a lucky little girl she was to be out of the damp valley heat of Gorham and surrounded by such lovely nature: pine trees, freshwater lakes, ocean. . . . Unfortunately, just as Janet got to the part about the daily fun on the beach Googie began to cry and Arthur had to push back his chair wearily and take her for a walk the way Daddy did with Mommy the other day. From his place beside Doris, a dainty feeder who ate with hooked pinky, Jason looked up pleasantly and said: "Guess what, Janet? I don't like franks anymore."

"Really?" Janet answered, turning down a sputtering little gas flame of rage—"Well, that happens to be *choucroûte garnie*, and I happen not to be a short-order cook," and turned it down again when Jason grinned chummily. She had inadvertently stumbled across an old family joke. "Daddy," Jason had said at seven, "are you going to marry Janet? I wish you would." And then: "Your *wife*? I thought she was your cook." Oh, I'm through with you, Janet thought, pushing back a drudge's damp lock of hair, and went outside to cool herself off on deck, leaving an ever darker and more retreating Doris to cope with the clearing up.

Somebody, Jason probably, had abandoned the binoculars without their case in the bulging seat of a striped canvas deck chair, and Janet put them on, scanning an unrewarding lowering sky before she let them drop heavily to her chest again. Unfortunately, in extolling the landscape to Googie in baby talk, she seemed to have extinguished it for herself. There it was, exactly as described, a beautiful darkening Indian pond with gulls silently gliding like black V's overhead, and in the distance a few twinkling lights and then a silhouette of spiky pine trees with a red ball of sun sinking down behind. But there was no joy in it anymore, no excitement, no peace, no pleasure in a child's voice suddenly echoing across the water. Yes, *through* with you, Janet repeated to herself, and almost in tears reminded herself that she *was* only dealing with a child after all, a lonely child, an awkward pre-adolescent. Not that she could blame herself too much for the intensity of her feelings, since what were they actually but a reflection of her intense feelings of love and loyalty toward poor Arthur, who even now was wending his way back slowly down below, carrying a dozing sweatered Googie over his shoulder, looking so spent and weary, poor soul, it was impossible to imagine him even having the strength to set up his dominoes later on. (She had promised Jason dominoes and he would have them.) And then, while Arthur was still trudging up the rickety outside stairway with his burden, the telephone began to ring indoors. Janet stayed where she was, gripped by a terrible foreboding.

". . . Hello, Mommy?" Jason said seriously. A sudden rush and rustle of wind obscured the rest of his thin young voice. Then it subsided and Arthur was on the line. Then there was a long and dreadful silence.

"To *me*?" Janet said when Arthur stuck his head out on deck to tell her she was wanted. She followed him inside with a sinking heart, reluctantly accepting the grim abrupt thrust of the receiver. Not that a call from Claire was in itself unusual or, really, anything to worry about. On the contrary. Jason and his mother had been talking to each other on the phone almost every day, and she had even encouraged him to call first, making merry little signs when it was time to cut it short and not run up a bill, though finding it odd that a thirteen-year-old boy should need to speak to his "Mommy" (he called her "Mommy") quite so often. But why couldn't Claire have skipped one night for a change? Also, where *was* everybody? Arthur had absurdly stalked off when she picked up the phone as if it were *she* who wanted to speak to Claire and not vice-versa, but Jason and Doris and even little sleepy Googie had also gone away to play some game, leaving her alone in an empty glassed-in living room. Claire's voice cut through her thoughts, amazingly matter-of-fact and reassuring.

"Oh, fine, thanks," Janet said, "and you?" astonished to find herself so suddenly calmed and humanized. ". . . No. No, I don't think it's anything to worry about either . . ." and with a guilty look around the deserted living room permitted herself a little laugh at Claire's amused suggestion that they both knew Arthur.

"Well, yes," Janet said, still laughing a bit, "but unfortunately *I* don't know what really brought on this silly business either."

Except, no, wait. Yesterday had been overcast, one of those hazy deceptive days when people lay around on the beach getting badly sunburned without even realizing it. Which was exactly what had happened—*her* fault, Janet supposed, except that she had been fooled by a gray sky too—and by evening they were all sick from overexposure, reeling around with chills, hot flushes, nausea, all the rest of it. "I mean, I slept in this old black sweater myself," Janet said. "Truly, I was shivering so much I thought I had the flu." Yes, and before that, when she and Arthur came back from their walk, Doris, the only one seemingly untouched, though she hurried over the thought, Doris had already smeared Noxema all over Googie's burning little red back and shoulders with the white crisscross strap marks. And by night, Arthur was walking around in a semi-crouch, unable to bend his knees, and—Claire's voice cut in again, still pleasant, still calm, still matter-of-fact, but patently uninterested—oh well, why should the minor agonies of the rest of them concern her?—with the suggestion that maybe *Janet* could speak to Jason if the occasion ever came up naturally since Arthur, *ha, ha*, was still sore as a boil. "Well, yes," Janet said, though she was no longer sure what the joke was about. (Actually, wasn't there some old one about the laughing hyena—intercourse two times a year, so why was he laughing?).... What? Not enough sleep? The poor kid (*ha, ha* again) thought the world was coming to an end if he didn't clock up his ten hours? But he had been clocking up eleven hours, Janet wanted to cry out, twelve, one night had even boasted of *thirteen*!

Instead, she contented herself with saying: "Well, I think you'd agree that we've been leading a pretty free-and-easy life here too," adding with a certain grim humor, "unless, that is, you regard Go-Fish as frenetic," and glanced first at the box of dominoes on the white formica table from which as she had imagined, Arthur had barely been able to extract a few dotted pieces, and then at Jason, who had just come sauntering back in to flop in a canvas sling chair and sit facing her, chubby legs thrust out, high sneakers and all. "Furthermore, I don't think he's sick now either," Janet continued speaking directly to Jason, who gave her a wary betrayed look, as if she had just crossed over to the other side, which she had, which he might as well get through his head once and for all. "I'm positive that the stomachache was the simple result of overexposure. However, if you'd like me to take him to the doctor, any-way...." She smiled into the receiver. "Oh, Claire, of *course*, I under-stand. I'm the one who's been urging him to keep in touch. No, I'm sure you don't, any more than we do.... No, not *secretly*. Goodness, I've always known when he called. I.... *Midnight*?" Janet said. "No, no I didn't know about *that* one," and hung up soon after, having prom-ised not to tell Arthur, who, yes, would be furious, and looked again at Jason, who quickly brought his knees together and sat up straight. Down the corridor the toilet flushed loudly, and then Googie's bare little feet padded her back to bed in her long flannel nightgown. Oh gallant Googie! Oh *Mama's* boy!

"But don't you see, Arthur?" Janet said in the bedroom, having sent Jason off to sleep immediately, and herself too, by mistake, while she was at it. "The point is that for *his* sake it's all so wrong. How will he ever be a man if—?"

Arthur put aside his detective story and looked up at her from their bed where he lay, on a large slab of varnished plywood with another slab of foam rubber on top of it for a mattress. His eyes were red-rimmed and bloodshot. Arthur, poor thing, was crying.

Well, nevertheless, damn it, in a way it was liberating having nothing more to lose. *Wasn't* it? Janet asked again as up ahead, Arthur nodded sadly to the suggestion and continued to plod on through the dense still woods, picnic basket in hand full of chicken and wine, food of their old and now their new freedom. Well, all right, maybe liberating wasn't quite the word to use the way things were going these days, even at Gorham. Still, Arthur could have been a bit chirpier. It was a hot muggy day, with tiny sand flies brought by an irritable east wind biting so tenaciously that Arthur kept killing several at a time with a single bloody hairy slap at an arm or a leg, like the little tailor in Googie's favorite story. But personally, she couldn't help feeling a sense of cool relief, a sense of swimming in the cool waters of her reclaimed privacy. No more picnics, no more books, no more Jason's dirty looks, though there had been one, at being left behind with Googie. Because whatever they did, he would hate it anyhow and go yammering to his mother. Which, while no doubt tragic, was, well, liberating. Smiling, she reached out to touch Arthur on the shoulder, and he patted her hand without looking around, and then turned in at the Schlumberger's driveway. Still without speaking (what need, with this tender married telepathy?), she followed him, Indian style, around toward the back of the small boarded-up house, hardly more than a shack really, which was its special charm, and flopped down on the tiny pond beach beside him, to sit cross-legged looking out. It was all almost painfully familiar, the view of the small round lake, with the two arms of pines embracing this scratchy spit of sand, and the peeling overturned blue rowboat, rope entangled in the scrub grass, and the clear brown water rippling and sudsing between rushes and lily pads, almost painfully reminiscent of other hot summer afternoons picnicking at this same spot, and nights swimming naked in black velvet water. *Velvet.* Suddenly the word took on a poignant foretaste of autumn in Gorham, of plaids and wools and furs in the small expensive shop windows on Green Street, and giddy girls going in and out. Pampered darlings, all of them, even the radicals in the jeans and tie-dye sweatshirts. She herself had never been one of the silly ones. Far from it. In fact it was her seriousness that had recommended itself to Arthur when he was looking for a graduate-student reader for the course he and Bob Carlsbad were teaching on Victorian morality. Still, what an awful loss. Only the second week of June and already the whole rest of the summer seemed only a long dusty road to the fresh excitements of September. She snuggled a bit closer to Arthur who, drumstick in hand, was staring straight ahead, and gradually some of the old magic of the place returned, a magic that the longer they sat there sipping the too-hot white wine and eating the too-cold chicken filled her with fond thoughts of dear Herman and Inge. Such a distinguished couple actually, the Schlumbergers, she a painter, he a correspondent for the *Frankfurter Zeitung.* There! Janet thought with a little thrill of self-justification. The crème de la crème of intellectual society, and *they* didn't regard it as torture to spend time with her and Arthur. Au contraire. (Why was she thinking in French?) In any case, she could well imagine herself saying to Jason in the near future and with a mocking smile that should put him in his place forever: "Odd as it may seem, Jason, many people consider it a privilege to be with us." Maybe not privilege. Maybe treat, on account of his age level? Aloud, she sighed, laying her head against Arthur's thin, touchingly vulnerable bare shoulder.

"Poor Googie."

"Googie?" Arthur said, screwing his head around. "What's the matter with Googie?"

"Oh, nothing, really, darling, I know that. She'll always triumph. I just suddenly realized how difficult all this must be for her. Our golden girl, our shining star, the center of our universe—suddenly displaced by that enormous sibling." She smiled ruefully and looked up—"Damn it, sweetheart, why can't even nonsociologists talk about children without using such jargon these days?"—but Arthur merely frowned off into the distance. Well, perhaps it wasn't fair to distract him with their shining success when he was brooding about his darkest failure.

"Not that I regret her having the experience, you understand, darling," Janet said. "Far from it. And not that au fond she doesn't want everything he has and vice-versa. I'm merely terribly impressed by how she's taking it. Not a peep, not a murmur. And really so ungrudging about sharing her position. I think that shows a terrific generosity of spirit, don't you?"

Overhead, Arthur gave a sad hmphing sound, like a bear being roused from a great sleep.

"I miss them up here," Arthur said.

"The Schlumbergers? Oh, yes, I too. I feel as if I were basking in an absolute legacy of goodwill."

"It's a cultural thing."

"Oh, yes, absolutely."

"The dirty bitch."

"Which dirty bitch, darling?"

"Your friend, Claire, whom you chat with so happily over the telephone."

"Arthur!"

"Oh, damn it, I'm sorry," Arthur said, quickly laying aside his drumstick and putting an arm around her. "Forgive me. I've just been feeling so lousy, that's all."

"I know, darling," Janet said, "I understand," and sighing deeply, thought a moment against his shoulder. "Sweetheart, listen—would you like *me* to talk to Jason? Find out what's really bothering him?"

"Could you?" Arthur said. "Would you?"

"Well, of *course* I could, of *course* I would," Janet said, drawing away, though not before touching Arthur's dear dark cheek tenderly. (In this respect, of course, Claire was right, tiny slights did tend to fester in his mind.) "Only, mightn't it do more harm than good? Play into his hand, so to speak?"

"In what respect?" Arthur said.

"Well, I mean, mightn't it divide us in his mind, so to speak, separate one from the other, which is probably exactly what he wants? Not that I'm not tempted to play the little mother and confidante, darling—of course, I am, how could I not be? But maybe, wouldn't it be better to have him understand once and for all that he can't have me without you? That wherever you are, I am, in this as in everything else? In short, that I'm your wife? Because by himself what could he possibly understand of marriage? After all, his mother has never taken another husband, so what could he know of the love and loyalty a woman can feel for a man? Of the tenderness, and . . . well, maybe it would be a good time for him to find out. Though, of course, if you do want me to talk to him—"

"No, you're absolutely right and I'm grateful," Arthur said. "I love you."

"And I love you."

They kissed, but with one eye each on the pond. The white wine had made them sweaty and sleepy, and overhead a shimmery white sun had moved clear of the grateful shade of the pine trees. ". . . oh, *Christ*, what a bitch," Arthur murmured, shaking his head, as they got up and left the prickly pine-needly patch of beach to stand toeing the clean rippling brown water.

"Actually," Janet said, pulling her tank suit down behind, "she sounded quite reasonable over the phone."

"Sure, as reasonable as a laughing hyena," Arthur said, through some married alchemy hitting on precisely the metaphor that had flashed through Janet's mind during the telephone call. "Why do you refuse to realize that behind that bland giggling façade lurks a woman who hates our guts?"

"Why hates our guts?" Janet said. "You didn't leave her for me or anything."

"Because, my dear, as I've explained to you ad nauseam, we are operating on entirely different cultural levels, that's why."

"Arthur, darling, there's no need to be angry with *me*," Janet said, laughing lightly and wondering if it wasn't just the sort of thing Claire might have said.

"Sorry," Arthur said, automatically. "But goddamn it, it makes me boil to think of that bitch in her fancy little East Side co-op, throwing parties for the Black Panthers and thinking that makes her some kind of a radical activist. I'd like to tell all those Huey Newtons of hers that all she really cares about is dough and 'good relationships' . . . 'Arthur, darling, Jason must learn the value of good relationships' . . . Do you realize that every stitch on that kid's back comes from Brooks Brothers? Do you realize that every stitch on *her* back comes from Bergdorf's?" Arthur swung around furiously, facing Janet but not seeing her. "And then that insipid pretense of despising the academy when she doesn't know a goddamn thing about it. When any real intellectual drives her frantic, makes her crawl with jealousy. Writhe with suspicion."

"She really didn't sound like that over the phone this time," Janet said.

"Okay, fine, have it your way," Arthur agreed, taking a casual breath and a further step or two into the water. "Only the next time you complain about the Betty Carlsbads of this world, maybe I'll be dubious too."

"All right, darling. Touché," Janet said. "But why now?"

"All I can tell you," Arthur said darkly, "is that the boy is being deliberately brought up to hate and despise us." But he doesn't despise *me*, Janet thought, wondering if this were a compliment or an insult. "Believe me, the day we took him out to Nauset Light and he said, '*big deal*,' I saw it all coming."

"But he's been with us before."

"All I can tell you," Arthur said, "is that tootsie is behind it somewhere, egging him on with those chatty little letters, and those chatty little phone calls that cost me a fortune."

"Oh, no, darling." Janet laughed. "That's where I know you're wrong. She doesn't at all want him to come home now. Far from it. She told me so over the phone."

"Oh?" Arthur said, turning to her with a sudden dark wiry look, almost a betel nut brown. "What else did she say?"

"Only that Jason had called her the night before at midnight, and scared her stiff. Which was why—"

"*Midnight?* What the hell does that little bastard mean, sneaking around, making long-distance calls in the middle of the night?"

"Oh, I know, darling," Janet said with a rueful smile and a shake of the head. "It's awful. I felt so demeaned when she told me, so socked in the solar plexus."

"And I'll bet that bitch had the nerve to tell you not to tell me—am I right?" Arthur demanded, plowing a straight furrow as usual.

"But I *did* tell you, darling," Janet said, "which is the real point, isn't it?" and as Arthur splashed angrily through the shallows until he sank down in the blue lake and swam, repeated a couple of more times: "Isn't it? Isn't it?"

Bright morning sun and sounds of another quarrel, this time between Arthur and Googie over whether there were real germs in wheat germ, Arthur saying *no*, and Googie crying: "Yes! Yes! Yes!" (Doris, the black mother's helper, had gone completely haywire in the past few days, and either lay inaccessible in her bottom bunk in Googie's room, or else lurked in the background, a dumb dark witness to whatever they didn't want her to see and hear.) And, as if this were not enough— "Go on, Googie," Janet heard Jason whisper from behind some thin wall—oh, damn these modern houses, so clean in design and weak on partitions—"Go on, Googie, *give* it to him." Janet sat up in bed in a fury. Oh, no, they lived here in peace and love. No filthy adolescent was going to teach *her* daughter his dirty tricks. And then, feeling that she had gone a bit too far in sexual allusion, calmed herself down and contented herself with saying to the air: "Cut that out, Jason, I heard you." "Okay," Jason's voice said.

She deliberately did not mention the episode to Arthur, who hardly needed it to inflame him anyway, since the midnight call to "Mommy" seemed to have been enough to set him off permanently—how strange to feel so apologetic toward Claire—and who all day long now alternated between icy calm and burning rage, like those fires of his in the living room grate that either kept going out or else burst into flame when they were all on their way to bed. For example, a typical incident yesterday on the beach:

Jason, idly filling a Coke can with sand: "Are you sure the timetable's right about when the plane leaves from Hyannis Port, Dad?"

Arthur, as in a Ring Lardner story: "Shut up."

Fortunately, Doris, who had turned out to be a phys. ed. major, was out of earshot, practicing black handstands against a white sky some little distance away. But a while later, as they were scrabbling back up the dunes loaded with gear toward where the new car stood parked and lonely, baked with red dust, Arthur burst out again: "So help me god, Janet, one of these days I'm going to haul off and sock him one." Why darling? Janet wondered, puffing uphill, bare legs scratched by the thin waving beach grass, that is, what had Jason done *this* time? Told Arthur to pick up his beach towel. Told or asked? Had he said please? "Treating me like a servant," Arthur muttered, plowing on ahead, ankle deep in the small Sahara, festooned with beach towels, laden with sand pails and other toys, so that when he turned around, his nose grazed the beak of Googie's duck-tube in passing. "Who the hell does he think he is? Who the hell does he think *I* am? Listen, do you know what he did this morning—?" Yes, she did know, but no, she couldn't possibly know what Arthur knew and vice-versa. "Left a little open postcard for me to mail on the kitchen counter. 'Dear Mommy—counting the hours until I see you!'" Yes, it was certainly very humiliating—she bent to sniff at a sweet new pink beach rose, disentangling her towel from the lower part of the bush. But hadn't they been counting the hours too? And wasn't a boy entitled to tell his mother he missed her? Suppose the shoe was on the other foot and it was Googie? And was it actually their business to read his outgoing mail? On the other hand, hadn't Jason left the postcard lying around just so they *would* read it? Oh, so many other hands—and feet. The problem was beginning to resemble that ridiculously pretentious stat-uette of Buddha that Betty Carlsbad kept spotlit on a teakwood book-shelf in Gorham, and that always seemed to be doing something else, supplicating in prayer, picking a nose, scratching an ear, depending on which two hands you were looking at. By coincidence the Carlsbads had just arrived at the Cape and asked them to dinner that night. So maybe had the time come to bring this tangle with Jason out into the open, put their own Buddha on display, as it were?

Unfortunately, out of misplaced kindness, the Carlsbads had also invited Jason to dinner. It was heartbreaking to leave Googie behind, silhouetted against Doris's mute, unfeeling black knees, weeping her heart out—"I hope you have a *mizzable* time!"—not out of naughti-ness but hurt pride, because when before Jason had it ever occurred to Googie that she ought to be asked to dinner parties? Squatting tenderly, Janet promised her a new toy "that only Googie" would play with (what could that be?) and then all during the drive to the Carlsbads further tortured herself trying to think of places where Googie could go and Jason couldn't, so that by the time she ushered him out of the car, she counted it all, no longer debating the rights and wrongs of the matter, as still another strike against him. Three more days, Janet thought, watching the grim irony of a beaming Betty and Bob standing proudly in the gloaming outside of their Cape Cod farmhouse, and Jason's response of a firm, little manly handshake. Three more days. True, the boy looked exceptionally well—as who wouldn't who had spent all that time grooming himself and spiffing himself up in the only bathroom? ("Arthur, darling, maybe *you* could get him out of there.")—and then emerged in a brand-new bleeding-madras jacket from Brooks Brothers (Arthur was right, she had looked at the label), fashionably worn jeans, mod boot-like shoes, and a shiny black hairdo with especially shiny long sideburns. And true that the Carlsbads could not be expected to realize that this comedy they had often enacted both in Gorham and at the Cape should suddenly overnight have turned into tragic farce. Still, it was hard not to remember that the Carlsbads were originally Arthur's friends, not hers, or to keep from asking herself how two people supposedly so intelligent and sensitive to nuance—she threw in Betty for the sake of argument—could miss the general bleakness of response. Actually, she had always liked Bob, a gentle serious scholar, already a bit prematurely fuddy-duddy except when he launched into one of his long Polish stories, the great hit of dinner parties in Gorham. It was Betty who stuck in her craw. Betty with her long blond page boy and bangs, and her hostess skirt, and the two houses, and the hysterical laugh that stopped all conversation dead. Actually, it was the two houses that were most irritating: (1) because they revealed that in spite of the apparent helplessness, Betty had a swift eye for real estate, (2) because more than anything else they reflected the prevailing, strangely shifting winds of Betty's mind. In Gorham, a modern architect's cliff-hanger, featuring the Buddha in the teakwood bookcase, and a study for Bob all in black leather including a chair that *faced* his desk, as if he were a doctor in a consulting room. Here, on the Cape, Betty's weird idea of rural Americana, consisting mostly of flotsam and jetsam sold to her by the alcoholic lady who ran the local antique shop: cane chairs, wicker chairs, rattan chairs, some painted white, some blue, stoneware washbasins planted with geraniums, an old upright piano, crisscross curtains with chenille pom-poms on the bottom, Victorian paperweights, a Civil War settee, fake colonial ancestors staring down from the wall along with still lives of dead glazed-eyed fish and waxen fruit, also, since it was Betty, a few pieces of frenzied driftwood, and a cut-down round marble table from the old Gorham house where the two couples sat after the usual gourmet dinner drinking brandy out of red souvenir glasses from Bradley Beach, 1905. Bob's Polish story had gone very well—"Judge, I kill wife. I kill man. Judge, must be *supper* on the table!"—and when they had all finished laughing, the children had been sent off to amuse themselves, Jason with amazing willingness, probably because it flattered him to be sandwiched between pretty Eloise Carlsbad in her miniskirt, who was actually Jason's age but a good head taller, and Bob's son Tom, a shaggy-headed snob who had been a troublemaker and a heartache even before this year when he had precociously managed to be kicked out of Yale as a sophomore. "Imagine!" Betty said with *that* laugh. "Only a sophomore," and it was all Janet could do not to tell herself as usual that this kind of heartache could have been avoided in a minute with a little affection and plain common sense. She looked longingly after Arthur, who was following Bob into a mid-Victorian study to look at an article about American society in the year 2000, and then she was left with a hostessy Betty twitching at a long paisley dirndl.

"Well, I'm afraid adorable isn't *quite* the word," Janet said, taking the plunge with a grim social smile and a sense of any port in a storm. "In fact, not to put too fine a point on it, he's been behaving like a perfect little bastard—" and then, having opened the floodgates (But why so many drowning metaphors? Eliot: "*Fear death by water*."), found herself saying yes to another brandy and suddenly telling Betty all about it, leaning forward to include dates and places, and sitting back again to end on what she realized was troubling her most, this increasingly intense, almost visceral antipathy between Jason and Arthur:

"—like a *gut* reaction, really."

Across the marble table, in a rattan peacock chair painted blue, Betty nodded and smiled—the first right thing she had done, since it not only indicated that she was sympathetic, but also that she didn't take the matter too seriously. "Oh, I know. Jason would have no trouble at all if he were alone with you."

"Really? Do you think so?"

"Well, of course. You don't fly off the handle every five minutes the way Arthur does—I think he's too rough on him, by the way. You don't get disturbed by every little crime the boy commits."

True. Perfectly true, in fact, but as she explained to Betty, having already explained to Arthur, surely the point nevertheless was that Jason had to get along with his *father*, that the two of them, man and boy, had to find some modus vivendi. "Actually," Janet added tentatively, "Arthur feels that it's basically a cultural problem—"and was amazed when Betty not only smiled in her blue peacock chair, but nodded even harder.

"—you know," Janet said, "the kind of basic yahoo antagonism between people like his mother and people—like us."

"Oh, yes, absolutely," Betty said. "I think it's obvious."

Obvious? Then why hadn't it been so obvious to Janet until Arthur made such a point of it? She dropped the matter quickly, not wishing to pursue it. Also, she was still feeling vaguely uneasy about the phrase "people like us," still half-waiting for Betty to demur, free her from this vague sense of self-betrayal.

"You see, the thing that startled me most," Janet said finally, changing the subject somewhat, "was that until that morning we were all so happy together. At least I thought we were. No, I *know* we were. One isn't wrong about such things. There was simply no tension. We were all of us terribly gay, free as air, laughing, telling little in-jokes. And while I can hardly put myself forward as a monument of quivering sensibility—" Pause. Betty sat intent in blond bangs and page boy. "—I just can't believe that if all this hostility were seething in him, I would have been impervious to it. Of course, it wasn't directed at *me*, that's true. It still isn't. But nevertheless, we *were* happy. I know we were."

"Of course you were," Betty agreed. "I imagine that's exactly what brought it on."

"You do?"

"Certainly. Not that I know too much about Jason's home life, aside from his mother."

"You know Claire?"

"Well, I met her once or twice when she and Arthur—" Betty began with an absurdly exaggerated air of diffidence, and then suddenly killed the subject with her wild social cackle.

"I can't say I particularly cared for her," Betty said soberly.

"Oh."

"But to get back to Jason—look, Janet, there he is, abandoned to maids most of the day—I take it she's still doing publicity for Warner Brothers?—leading a typically tense New York existence. And then he comes up here and sees the warm easy life people like us lead, and naturally he loves it, which inevitably sets up a conflict."

There it was again, that ubiquitous "people like us"—could Betty possibly consider herself an *intellectual*? From there, after another round of brandy in the red Bradley Beach souvenir glasses ("They're really rather charming, actually." "She has none left," Betty said quickly, guarding her find), from there it was an easy step for Betty to confide her own problems with Tom—and why shouldn't she?—complaining with an obvious, giggling pride that Tom had not only joined the Weathermen, against Bob's express prohibition, but also stoned the Justice Department in November, and it was all Janet could do not to cry out that with a little affection, a little common sense that boy could have been kept away from Washington! Still, riding back home later along Gull Pond Road, all three in front, Janet between Jason and Arthur on the cold dark leather seat, they seemed to be once more united by the old sweet feeling of camaraderie. Maybe it was only that a country night softened sharp edges, but Betty's idea that Jason had been *too* happy with them was suddenly very touching, very persuasive. Even Arthur, bent over the steering wheel to concentrate on the thick yellow swath of headlights cutting through fog, seemed less prickly than usual, more absorbed, less *personal*. They had joked about Googie's red-faced rage at being left behind, and promised to do something in the morning to make it up to her. Then they said what a sweet man Bob was—marvelous Polish story, where had he picked up that accent?—and that Betty was really very sweet too in her own way, besides being a first-rate cook, and Jason, who had managed to pack it away in spite of the "upset stomach" said she sure was, and what was the name of what they had eaten?

"Boeuf en daube, I *think*," Janet said, laughing. "They're both crazy about you, you know, Betty called you *adorable*," and looked around, laughing again, when Jason gave a little chuckle and a shrug. "What did you all do after dinner?"

"Oh, we just sat around the kitchen reading *Mad* and playing poker, and kidded around about sex," Jason said. "She's nice, Eloise."

"Yes, she's a lovely girl."

"She offered me a kitten."

"Really? Did you hear that, Arthur? Eloise offered him a kitten, isn't that sweet? What a shame you won't be able to take it, Jason, on account of going to Switzerland."

"Yeah," Jason said.

They got out of the car, laughing when their lights froze a black-eyed raccoon nosily pawing through their garbage, and climbed up on deck, still united by their good time at the Carlsbads' and the stars drifting like pinpoints through the dark gray clouds overhead. As a special treat, a vestige of the old special treats Janet used to think up to make Jason feel there were advantages to being older than Googie, they let him stay up with a glass of ginger ale while they each had a nightcap of scotch and water. Then Jason began to blink, and Janet sent him gently off to bed, remembering his pride in clocking up sleep like an achievement. She remained with Arthur at the white formica table, peacefully listening to Jason's usual bedtime noises, the thump of pillows and spread landing on the floor, much gurgling and splashing in the bathroom. Then Jason came padding back in his creased pink flannel pajamas to wish them both good night, and after a pause, wish them both good night again, giving Janet a quick toothpasty kiss on the cheek and extending a manly hand to Arthur.

"Good night, Dad."

"Good night, son."

"Dad?"

"Yes, sweetie?"

Jason took a crumpled timetable from his flannel breast pocket.

"I just wanted to remind you," he said, not so much consulting the thing as holding it out as evidence, "that the plane leaves Hyannis at nine thirty A.M."

Janet closed her eyes. ". . . I am well aware of what hour your plane leaves," she heard Arthur say, as from a great distance. "I can assure you that the time is engraved on my heart. As it is, I assume, on yours."

"What are you blowing a fuse about?" Jason said. "I just wanted to remind you."

She followed Arthur into the bedroom. "Arthur," Janet said, ". . . *darling*—please put down that detective story for a minute—I've been talking to Betty."

"Betty Boob," Arthur said, unexpectedly not furious. Sighing, he sat down on their thin slab bed and stared at the night through the sightless black picture window. "—I talked to Bob."

"Oh? Really, darling? What did he say?"

"I'm not sure. Something about a phase all adolescents go through, like *their* loony kid." Arthur lay back with his hands folded behind his head, elbows out, eyes closed, listening, like an analyst who had somehow found himself on the couch: "Okay, let's hear it from the Cackler."

"—well, she had a feeling that maybe he was *too* happy with us—" Janet began, and stopped short, drooping inside, and wondering how Betty's inane theory could ever have sounded plausible even without the sight of Arthur lying there, nodding grimly away at the ceiling.

"*Too* happy with us," Arthur repeated. "Oh, that's great. That's just marvelous. So now we have exactly nine thousand informed theories on why my own kid thinks his father is his *worst enemy!*"

"Arthur—he'll hear you."

"Hear me?" Arthur said with a hysterical laugh. "You expect my son to hear *me?*"

It did not surprise either of them when at breakfast the next morning Jason remarked that Eloise was boy crazy and that she had tried to palm off a kitten on him, since for the time being they had simply written the boy off as lost. Besides which, as Arthur pointed out, it was exactly the kind of slyness, the gift for the stealthy about-face that the boy had inherited from his mother. What did surprise Janet was the sudden depth and loyalty in her feelings for the Carlsbads—yes, good old Betty Boob too—so that when for the fifth or sixth time Jason pulled out the tattered timetable that he evidently slept with, Janet said with unconcealed asperity and a glance at Arthur, "Believe me, Jason, we're as anxious to see you on that plane as you are." Except there was no relief in it, no satisfaction, because Jason put the timetable back in his wallet and said seriously, "Thanks, Jan."

No, no relief, no satisfaction of any kind, no point at which one could look back and say, "*There's* a job well done." No, and again it didn't surprise Janet in the least that the very first evening that she and Arthur were finally going out by themselves to their first cocktail party of the season, at the Epsteins', who were very near, just the first right after the tree with the Indian signs, *that* was the moment that Claire would choose to call, and Jason would inform her in a piping choir boy's voice that Daddy and Janet were just on their way out and that he was having frozen pizza pie for dinner. So there it was. In the twinkling of an eye, ten days, almost two weeks, of prime roasts, steaks, chops, clever casseroles, up the chimney, sunk without a trace, vanished into thin air, as if in devouring them all inch by inch and voraciously, Jason had caused them never to have existed. It was all she could do not to grab the telephone from Jason's hand and tell Claire about each meal, giving her recipes, cooking times, ingredients, describe the mountains of onions chopped so fine the smell never left her hands, and the vats of meat coated with flour and browned interminably, and about defrosting before breakfast, and peeling and cutting, and having her sunglasses coat over with steam and blind her when she lifted the lid off a pot roast, of silver-foil baked potatoes snatched from the oven with burnt fingers, of endlessly stirring rizottos that stuck to the bottom of the pan, and racing back from the beach in a wet bathing suit to turn a coq au vin down to simmer, of packages and boxes of cookies carried back from the First National to be chewed to a paste, of endless quarts of milk and cans of soda, and bushels of apples, grapes, peaches, plums, cherries, whose stones and pits Jason left spat into open napkins and all the clean ashtrays, and finally of the fact that even the frozen pizza pie was a special treat because Jason said his mother always let him have one on Saturday nights. But what was the use, especially since as Arthur said, as they rode bucking and dragging along the sandy road, "What the hell business did she have asking him what he was having for dinner in the first place?"

Asking him? Janet wondered, fiddling with an earring, and smoothing down the long paisley skirt she had bought at the new homosexual boutique in the village. Yes, she distinctly remembered a pause before Jason said, in that ingenuous piping voice, "Frozen pizza pie." Actually, the answer was obvious. Claire was his mother.

"So she's his mother," Arthur said. "Big deal."

"Oh, but Arthur, look at it this way. How would *we* feel if we sent Googie off to stay with somebody and she called in the middle of the night to say she was sick and miserable? Frankly, I must say that I doubt that I'd behave with half of Claire's restraint—though as you pointed out, restraint is what she considers her strong suit. Personally, I'd probably fly up in the first plane and take Googie back immediately." The fallacy, as Janet realized as soon as she had uttered it, lay in the word "somebody." "Stay with somebody." As if Arthur were just *somebody* to Jason, anybody. Fortunately, however, though Arthur was very quick to feel such slights, Babs Epstein came running out barefoot in her Pucci pajamas, and he had no time to notice.

It was a brilliant, sunburned, noisy party, and they stayed as long as they damn pleased, wandering upstairs and down, indoors and out, from the upper mesh-enclosed deck to the lower open one, admiring the clever design of the Epsteins' new house, which, like a small summer version of the Whitney, was gray and had interesting slits for windows and was built upside-down: bedrooms in the dark below, living room with leather and chrome and Breuer chairs high on top, Japanese kitchen floating in limbo in between—greeting old friends ("Any new developments?" Betty Carlsbad asked so eagerly she failed to notice what Janet suddenly did, the similarity in skirts. . . . "*Süss!*" Inge Schlumberger exclaimed when told about the "pine-winey," Faulkner's phrase, picnic à deux), meeting some fascinating new people, writers, more analysts than last year, the Epsteins' architect, an avant-garde film-maker, Arthur Schlesinger, quite a few painters, including a young black, and a small disgruntled group from Harvard, one of whom Arthur claimed to know but who snubbed them anyway, and, having brought the problem with Jason out into the open once, felt sufficiently liberated to do it again, and again, terribly interested in everybody's interest—oddly, Babs Epstein, who was Inge's dealer in New York, was particularly keen and fascinated—so that Arthur's nine thousand theories became at least ten thousand. Which, as Janet pointed out, leaning her head against Arthur's shoulder during the swerving ride home, was certainly, and at the very least, a tribute to the ingenuity of their friends.

No, no satisfactions at all—Dr. Franzblau, a man, no relation, had nodded his grave professional agreement—and, meditating into her coffee cup with both hands around it the next morning, Janet decided once and for all to stop looking for them. All she asked now in the last few days before Jason got on that plane was a little peace—"Try to remember that this is my vacation too, Jason. I may not go out to a job, but I happen to work very hard all year also"—and she simply could not understand why Arthur refused to settle for a last few days of peace too, and instead continued to stalk the boy everywhere, a hot-breathed sleuth, snooping around for evidence of disrespect, lèse majesté, and inevitably finding them every place. "Get off my back, willya?" Jason shouted almost all day long, and Arthur triumphantly shouted back, "Don't talk to *me* like that, pipsqueak!"

"Look, my darling," Janet said, leading Arthur out onto the deck one noon just before he came to a boil, "perhaps it's none of my business, and if you think so, please tell me so outright. And also understand that I'm not debating the fundamental rights or wrongs of the situation, which are certainly all on your side."

"But?"

"But—I think you're too rough on the boy." A direct quotation from Betty, though she knew better than to attribute it. "He's right about one small thing, you know, darling. You don't get off his back. I mean that, given his present state of mind, it's inevitable that if you keep after him looking for something wrong you'll always find it. But I do think that a lot that you ascribe to the fact that he hates you because you divorced his mother, is universal to any child. I mean, think of all the things Googie goes around saying like 'stupid dumbhead' that don't make you angry because you know that she loves you and doesn't mean them personally. You know? Well, couldn't much of this also be true of Jason? And by blowing up every incident, aren't you playing right into his hands, handing him his grievances on a silver platter, as it were? Because of course what he's dying for is to be fussed over on *any* terms. Except that speaking frankly, Arthur, if you don't mind my speaking frankly, I'm really quite tired of fussing over Jason. I have a life of my own that I wouldn't mind getting back to. Also, I'm just too *old* to have the emotional temperature of my days and nights determined by the idiotic moods of a thirteen-year-old. I don't care who he is. Or what he is. Googie doesn't have this power over us and she never will have."

"Poor sweet," Arthur said, crestfallen and miserable. "It's been a lousy time for you."

"Lousier for you."

"No. You've always been so wonderful to him, and now he goes and spits in your face."

"Oh, well, no, Arthur, I don't really think he—"

"And you haven't had a chance to do any work, either."

It was a subject that she wished Arthur hadn't brought up. Only that morning there had been a letter from Arthur's Boston publisher regretting that her opening chapter and outline, while certainly interesting, was alas not sufficient to warrant . . . (also at Arthur's suggestion, she had submitted the opening chapter, without outline, to the *Texas Quarterly* and the *Kenyon Review*, both of whom had turned it down also, in almost the same words) . . . and she had been too busy defrosting and browning and chopping to feel good and miserable about it, or even to mention it to Arthur. Also Jason had been watching her closely, first trying to read over her shoulder and then trying to read her face, so that she had been suffering from acute emotional claustrophobia all day. I don't even have enough room to feel miserable with that kid around all the time, Janet thought, and also felt, unfairly maybe but felt it nevertheless, that if she hadn't been so busy attending to *his* needs, maybe this one of her own might have been satisfied.

"Oh, well," she said, "only three more days to D-day."

"Two and three-quarters," Arthur said, laughing too, but still unable to unhitch himself from the subject of Jason's perfidy. "No, to make *me* suffer like this is one thing. But to make you suffer is unforgivable."

Since she was feeling sorry for herself anyway, why not acknowledge the insult and receive the consolation?"

"Well, it's as you say," Janet began sadly. "Evidently, Claire's behind it all. And as you know, I've suffered from that sort of woman all my life—selfish, silly, mundane and proud of it. Bounded by the pettiest of considerations. Terrified by the imagination and the spirit. I mean you should hear Betty Carlsbad's tone of voice when she asks about my nah-vel. And always so proud of themselves, which is what really kills me. They really do think that because they're, quote, so practical and reasonable that they manage 'real life' so well while the rest of us, who try for something more, sort of muddle around it. I mean, really, when you think of it, the implication is actually rather infuriating. Claire's idea that because *her* mind is so mundane and lackluster, so exclusively concerned with superficialities, that this presumably makes *her* a great mother and homemaker, while *I* presumably let my child roam around in the streets like a wild animal. No, Arthur, really, the more I think about it the madder I get. I mean, where the hell does *she* get off feeling so smug about herself? She never even sees that boy from one end of the day to the next, and do you remember that weekend last spring when he came for the weekend with burns all over his arms, and she left him alone to heat up a frozen chicken pie for his dinner and the damn stove blew up on him? Well, novelist or not, *my* child doesn't have to heat up lonely frozen chicken pies for supper while I make merry for Warner Brothers, and she never will. And *my* child isn't petty and mean and sneaky and sullen. She's a brave gallant happy little girl, rosy-cheeked and smiling, and the world is her oyster and she eats well and goes to bed on time and she's healthy and well behaved and well brought up and I'd match her against anybody anytime."

"Hey, take it easy," Arthur said.

"Why should I? Who the hell is *she* to imply that because I work toward something more than money and publicity, even if I fail sometimes, that I'm incompetent? 'Well, of course *we* lead a very free and easy life,'" Janet mimicked bitterly. "What does she think *we* do? Beat these kids with whips? Use them for drunken orgies?"

"Take it easy," Arthur repeated, looking worried.

"But *why*, Arthur, *why*?" Janet cried. "Or is it all right for *you* to be insulted on a cultural basis, but not me? Am I not significant enough?" Oh, it's that damn publisher's letter burning a hole in my pocket, Janet thought, why don't I shut up? Oddly, it was Jason who ended what might have been a quarrel. The ubiquitous Jason, sliding open the glass doors to the deck, sniffing around, wanting to know what everybody was going to do today. They turned to him in a white glare of sunlight, stony-faced and stricken dumb. And this, Janet thought grimly, is the first good turn that brat has ever done me.

On the morning of Jason's departure, everybody expected to feel something and nobody did. Maybe because it was just too early: seven A.M., and it was *supposed* to be their vacation, and it was the Cape and outside it was raining. But there they all sat, shrouded in gloom, foggy-eyed, sticky-minded, passing intermittent yawns from one to the other, except for Jason who had evidently risen at dawn to prepare himself for flight, and sat there all dressed up in his madras jacket, black hair shiny with water, the alert stranger at the breakfast table. "Are you sure you have your ticket?" Arthur said, for perhaps the eighth or ninth time, and Jason sighed and said yes, it was in his wallet, and Arthur said where, show me. Whistling exasperatedly through his teeth and shaking his head, Jason reached into the inner breast pocket of the Brooks Brothers jacket and then shot Janet a sudden imploring look. Wrong wallet. The right wallet, naturally, was in the back pocket of his dirty blue jeans, which naturally lay at the bottom of his suitcase, where Janet had packed them away for him the night before. Naturally. Dousing a weary cigarette in her coffee, and holding together a rumpled Japanese kimono, Janet knelt on the floor beside Jason's plaid bag, which was already at the door, and fished around in between his sandy laundry and high ankle sneakers and the snorkeling equipment until she found the wallet and tossed it over to Jason at the table. She ignored the childishly grateful look as she had ignored the beseeching one, and sat down again. The wrinkled kimono, the cigarette butt drowned tan at the bottom of her coffee cup were extremely uncharacteristic of her, as she perfectly well knew. In fact all other days during Jason's stay, she had made a point, since he was so obviously an impressionable young male, of appearing at the breakfast table neat and clean and fully dressed. But today, she had perversely almost wanted to *afflict* him with her appearance, wipe out all those stupid heady hot whispered compliments about leg makeup commercials and all the rest of that TV nonsense. Except that Jason didn't seem to have noticed the difference, which maybe was just as well. In fact, it was Jason's immaculateness that offended, as, calm again now that his precious wallet had been restored, he sat whistling, drumming his fingers on the table, and in general trying to irritate Arthur into leaving early, the last of many insults and one to which Arthur, casually helping himself to more Sunkist raisins out of the red box and sprinkling them on his wheat germ, no longer responded. "You *mustn't* go! I have to *marry* you!" Googie cried, hitting herself on the head with her cereal spoon, but even she was easily deflected by the promise of a beach picnic with Doris if the weather cleared, or, if it didn't, a nice cozy weenie and marshmallow roast in the living-room fireplace using untwisted wire hangers for toasting forks. Did Jason notice how rapidly the sands were filling in the hole of his departure? If so, again he didn't show it. Oddly, only black Doris the mother's helper, was reacting as they had expected themselves to react, and stood hunched over the kitchen sink, head averted, as if she were hiding her tears. But maybe it was only an illusion, an atypical quirk of bad posture. Or maybe she was reacting the way she thought she was being paid to react. Who knew? Anyway, it made no difference.

But it *ought* to make a difference, Janet thought as the moment for departure drew near, and Arthur and Jason engaged in their last little hassle, about who would carry the suitcase. Arthur won. Jason got to have the raincoats over his arm. I ought to feel something for this child. Pity maybe. Or at least the sheepish goodwill of old enemies when the fight ends in a draw. Because he was only a child after all, only thirteen, not such a great age to take on a whole family and try to beat it to the ground. Why wasn't she moved to tears by this last sight of him in the doorway, all neat and shiny in the madras jacket and wet-combed hair, arm burdened with raincoats, his left eye twitching with anxiety, an old tic, as he waited to bridge that long gap between his mother and father, three hours by car and plane but light-years culturally, all by himself. But it was no use, and to be honest about it she didn't try very hard. Her only feeling was relief at last, and that she had earned this relief, at last. She put her hand on Jason's shoulder to say good-bye, and then at the last moment drew back and decided not to kiss him after all. Not out of coldness, but because she had suddenly become painfully aware of her too-early cigarette smell and the fact of her wrinkled Japanese kimono. In fact, she could hardly wait for them to leave so that she could take a shower, and the moment the dusty red Volvo lurched down the driveway—Arthur's driving always mirrored his emotional complications; not his fault, he was a New Yorker and had learned late—she took a long one, realizing with a sudden burst of delight as she dried herself off that the crush in the bathroom was over. For example, it was always possible for her to bathe while Arthur shaved, or brush her teeth over the sink while Googie sat on the toilet. (Exactly when Doris stole in to relieve herself remained mysterious.) Whereas Jason not only needed to use the entire bathroom by himself, but also made a point of hogging it for unbelievable periods of time. It was only a small blessing, this sudden freedom of the john, but the first accruing from Jason's departure, and she could not help rejoicing in it, just as when she came out of the bedroom dressed in a neat blouse and shorts, she found Doris rejoicing at finally being able to take over Jason's room. The second best room in the house, actually, now that Janet saw it without all the adolescent welter of *Mad*, discarded T-shirts and underpants, plastic baseball batting set, kites, etc., etc., but in the first happy flush of arrival she had promised it to Doris as soon as Jason's two weeks were over. (Googie, happily carrying a small silver transistor radio on top of a pile of *Modern Love* from Doris's old quarters to the new, hardly seemed to care that her room was dark, and so cramped with double-decker beds that there was hardly any floor space left to play on.) Suddenly Janet remembered how on that same first day while they were still wandering through the premises, Jason had said, "Hey, Janet, can I have the big room with the

ANN BIRSTEIN

windows on the lake?" and how she had hesitated and felt guilty, it was
so obviously the master bedroom, until Arthur intervened and said
certainly not. The thin edge of the wedge, the first tentacle shot out
by the octopus, she should have recognized it immediately for what it
was. "Can I help you?" Doris said, a mother's helper again, emerging
all smiles with Googie trailing behind, and uttering her first intelligible
words in about a week. No, but since the day had suddenly and mirac-
ulously cleared—true, Cape Cod weather was notoriously changeable,
but why not accept a sign from above when it came along?—suppose
Doris took Googie off on a nice little beach picnic?

Perfect. It was a return to their old lovely schedule of work in
the morning, play with Googie and do errands and marketing in the
afternoon. Janet wandered ecstatically throughout the house, finding herself absentmindedly standing in the middle of a room without
knowing how she got there—my god, how squalid that *Modern Love*
did look sprawled backside up on Jason's ex-bed—picking up Googie's
toys here and there, returning an old *Saturday Evening Post* left by a
previous tenant to the shelf underneath the cocktail table, where Jason
had found it in the first place, periodically returning to the deck where
she lifted her face to the warm sun. She felt serene and whole again,
a kaleidoscope whose pieces had finally jiggled into place, too happy
really to do more with the book at present than arrange Chapter I and
Outline on the ledge in the bedroom that had been her dressing table
and would now act as her desk, and give them a glance from time to
time. The other small cloud on the horizon, that Arthur would come
home dejected and miserable, as he always did after returning Jason,
was still hours away. She steeled herself to be sympathetic, though it
would be a wrench, she felt so beautifully Jason-free, and not resent
Arthur's need of her. Meanwhile there was still plenty of time to continue roaming blissfully about—but my god, could a college girl, even
a phys. ed. major from Tuskegee really read such crap?—thoughtfully
leaf through the first few pages of Chapter I, and then put on her bathing suit and lie out on deck for a while, smearing suntan cream on
her face and legs, or at least what little of it Jason had left, and then sit
up again, sweating, so absorbed in doing nothing, really, that it was
a shock when she finally decided to come inside and cool off again

to find Arthur already sitting at the kitchen counter, coffee cup and mail at his elbow, intent on the New York *Times*. How extraordinary that she hadn't even heard him drive up. True that the sandy driveway tended to muffle sound, but given the fact of Arthur's driving when disturbed—not his fault, of course. . . .

"How did it go, darling?" Janet said lightly, stepping around him to get some of Jason's leftover Kool-Aid out of the refrigerator. "No last-minute bombshells?"

"If there were I didn't notice," Arthur said, reading down one column and up the next. "I was too sleepy."

"You're emotionally exhausted," Janet said. "I think you ought to take a nap."

"I can't," Arthur said, closing up the newspaper and pushing it away, "I have too much work to do," and with a sigh, scooped up his mail and prepared to get down from the stool.

"Don't you want something to eat first, darling? More coffee?"

"No, that's okay," Arthur said. "Go on back to work, sweetie, I'm sorry I disturbed you."

"You didn't," Janet said. "Really. I've done what I wanted to, more or less, anyway."

"Really?" Arthur said, shaking his head. "Boy, do I envy you. I'll probably be at it until four, at least. Let's take a walk later, okay?"

"Arthur—" She watched him open the back door that led to the rickety outside steps and his studio/garage, feeling that something more needed to be said, but not sure what. "—Arthur, listen, it's going to be a beautiful day."

"It is already," Arthur said, turning with an amazingly, almost distressingly, boyish smile. "Well, old pal, mission accomplished. Although, my god—what we're going to do next year I don't know."

"We'll have him here again. Whether he likes it or not. And he'll stay his full time. And we'll do it year after year until he grows up or we all drop dead."

"I don't know," Arthur said, on his way out of the kitchen again with his mail, "I was thinking more in terms of Europe next summer."

Europe—with Jason?

* * *

81

At first the new schedule seemed to take firm hold. Each morning, Doris, now human and thoughtful, woke early and played quietly with Googie until breakfast time—"You see? Even she sensed the tension," Janet said, turning to Arthur as they lay in bed awakened by the smell of bacon and coffee in the cold country air—and then, having washed the dishes and tidied up in general took a devoted, no, adoring Googie, off on one of their picnics, by which time Arthur, returning from his morning walk in a brown cloud of concentration, was entering his study on the garage level to remain there until lunch, when he appeared at the kitchen counter already eager to have it done with and drive into town for the newspaper and the mail. Only for Janet wasn't it quite that easy—though to do herself justice she had always had a certain impatience with routine—and each day the number of new pages in the *ms.* had petered off to the extent that by now it was practically a daily toss-up whether to give it another whack, or go off to a part of the beach where Googie and Doris weren't. After all, it was supposed to be *her* vacation too, wasn't it? Janet thought, rising irritably from the dressing table desk on which a few bottles and jars had begun to make their reappearance—actually only some hand lotion, a little 4711 Kölnisch Wasser to soothe the wrists. And after all, wasn't she as entitled to rest and relaxation as anyone else, she continued, going out onto the deck, uncertain whom she was arguing with but resentful nevertheless. Not of Arthur, of course, happily occupied in the studio/garage down below, though to tell the truth in a strange way she had begun to miss him. Because now that Jason was gone—and hadn't it all rolled off his shoulders a little too easily?—Arthur seemed to have become an entirely new man, or rather reverted to the entirely old one; an Arthur who, considering the brevity of his absence, was surprisingly unfamiliar: cheerful, absorbed, able to slip from work into sleep into bright sunlight without missing a beat, without a flurry of the hesitation that plagued her constantly; an Arthur who, as he happened to be doing at the moment, would wander out into the driveway, take a deep breath of freedom like Chéri at the end of *Chéri*, and disappear back inside again; who when he really wanted to relax, simply walked off into woods by himself, or else got into the red Volvo and shot off godknew-where and without so much as a by-your-leave, and usually just when she had been meaning to go into town for groceries. An Arthur, in short, who was completely his own had fallen in love with and married and still loved—yes, of course she still loved him. So what indeed, she wondered, listening to a far-off noon siren—too late now to do any work before lunch—was there any argument about?

Back inside the house, she went directly into the kitchen where, more out of old habit and for the honor of the thing than because Arthur actually knew what he was eating these days, she made a fancy crab meat salad for lunch, not realizing until she had finished that it was exactly what they ate when Arthur's Boston publisher took them to one of his dreadful posh New York expense account restaurants, starting off the meal with his four or five old-fashioneds. She put the platter in the middle of the counter where Arthur even in his present mood would find it hard to overlook, and sat down to wait for him. On a private culinary basis, of course, she had lost Arthur completely. But then, she had never really had him there, had she? The gay silly times when they had *both* tootled off to the First National to purchase a few minutes' privacy with fifty dollars worth of groceries like the lovers in that *New Yorker* cartoon—they had gone completely, as she had known they would from the start. The Gorham Arthur would never have done it in the first place. He had merely been trying to help her with his son, ease the burden of a summertime child, which was only right and natural. Except, Janet suddenly thought, didn't this imply that Googie and all that went with her, the baby-sitters, the meals, the dirty clothes, the picking up the messes on the floor, the baths at bedtime were only *her* responsibility, not his? But then again, he had never helped her with Googie, *never*. Not even when she had gotten up for two bottle-feedings a night in a cold country house, exhausted to the point of hysteria. (It was some curious domestic point of honor in Gorham that there should be no baby nurses available, or practically any other household niceties, except for the gourmet cooking and home-ironed shirts.) No, she could go even further back, Arthur had never even once rubbed her back when she was pregnant, and in fact had even hurried her along, and in the bitter wintertime too, so anxious not to be late for some dinner party at the Carlsbads, or some stupid symposium at Truslow Hall, that top-heavy as she was at the time, all it required was one false move on the ice, a misstep, a twisted ankle and—"Hey, lady," one of the more drunken symposia panelists had once told her, "you shouldn't let him drag you by the arm like that. One of my sisters had a miscarriage that way."—oh, it was all she could do not to race downstairs to Arthur's study and rage at him with bitter, still unshed tears. Instead, she told herself to calm down and, elbows on the counter, eyes slightly narrowed, waited patiently until Arthur made his regular noontime appearance and, as she had expected, ate the entire crabmeat salad in a few bites, standing up, having pushed aside the garnish of green pepper rings and the rosette radishes right at the start:

"Arthur, I miss you," Janet said.

"What's the matter?" Arthur asked sympathetically, starting off with a hand over his favorite coffee mug. "More trouble with Chapter II?"

"Now look here, Arthur darling," Janet said, giving a sharp crease to a paper napkin before she stood up. "I really can do without your proprietary interest in my work, you know. It's true that people sometimes assume that I'm your former student, but as you're well aware I already had six credits toward my masters when we met, and they weren't in sociology, either."

"Hey, don't blow a fuse," Arthur said, laughing over his shoulder, and went back downstairs again to finish work and go off to town after that precious mail of his, about which when they were away from Gorham any length of time she had even known him to have nightmares of choked letter boxes. But she had never said "Don't blow a fuse," had she? A phrase which, as Arthur knew perfectly well, was not only a direct quotation from Jason but also, which maybe Arthur didn't realize, practically his only reference to the boy, direct or indirect, since the child had left. Which was surely odd, wasn't it, even from a certain point of view horrifying, considering that for nearly two solid weeks they had eaten, drunk and slept Jason day and night? And also what was more, that Arthur and Jason even looked so peculiarly alike: starting with the long nose and the straight black Indian hair, though Arthur's hair, as Jason never tired of pointing out, wasn't so black anymore, right on through that small blunt triangular torso that she always used to think of as Etruscan but wouldn't stay Etruscan long if Arthur kept insouciantly eating his way through entire plates of crab-meat salad with an adolescent pride in his appetite, straight on down to those pillar-like legs that started off shapely enough at the thighs and then went straight into the sneakers without any ankles at all. Not that, resemblance or not, at the rate he was going Jason would be half the man his father was. And not that Arthur needed ankles. Nobody *needed* ankles. And of course with or without them, Arthur was still—why still?—a very attractive man. The only criticism being possibly that as a serious intellectual—one of the attractions that had made her fall in love with him in the first place—Arthur tended to look his best in ordinary suits, in a dinner jacket, divine, and that casual beach wear, including the striped terry-cloth jacket-and-shorts combination that she had bought for him on Green Street, was not strictly up his alley, especially when he wore it with maroon silky socks, claiming itchy toes. It was a tremendous relief when Arthur, who really was very attractive, and happened to be wearing nice chino pants and a blue work shirt, came back with the mail and the paper and wanted to know if she wanted to go to the beach.

"You look upset," Janet said.

"I? No," Arthur said.

"Do you mind if I take a look at that bill from the telephone company?" Janet said, struck by a sudden chilling hunch.

"Go ahead," Arthur said, taking a renewed interest in *The New York Times*, which he spread out on the table and read bending over it with his hands in his back pockets, like President Kennedy in one of those last photographs in *Look*.

"—oh, my god."

"Yes, I know," Arthur said.

"And this only includes his first week."

"Yes, I know," Arthur said.

"And take a look at *this* item. Six dollars and thirty-two cents. That must be the famous cri de coeur to Mommy. Arthur, that's incredible! And this from a child so tight-fisted and money-mad he wouldn't even share the bottle-deposits with Googie."

"I know," Arthur said. "Don't you want to get your suit on?"

"But, Arthur, darling, don't you *care*?"

"Of course I *care*," Arthur said. "But he's not returning bottles now, so what's the use of talking about it?"

"But, darling, there's a principle involved. What kind of future can a thirteen-year-old have who's so indulged he can't even live a week without talking over twenty-three dollars' worth to his Mommy? My god, Arthur, think of your own childhood."

"I do," Arthur said, "constantly," and sighing deeply, sat down at the white formica dining table, once bloodied and busy with food and family argument, now antiseptic and empty, except for his newspaper and the small pile of mail. "But what can I do? That bitch has practically turned him into a hippie already." He flailed an arm in the direction of the *Times*. "I'm worried sick. Look at the Tate murders."

"Oh, Arthur," Janet said, starting to laugh, then changing her mind. "No, really, n'exagérons pas. Hippies are said to be very gentle people."

"Bullshit," Arthur said dismally. "The kid's dooomed."

Bullshit. Doom. Ironic that two such words should release Arthur from his long, unnatural silence. But now he began to talk about Jason as he always used to from the time when they were first married, no, from the time when they first met, particularly when he had just returned Jason after a visit—which had started so far back Jason would toddle to the table in his cowboy hat, parking his gun on the washing machine—telling of his hopes for the boy (very few), his misgivings for the child's future, all his old trepidations, so that listening to him Janet suddenly and inexplicably felt herself filled with pity for the child, with all the emotion she had tried so hard to feel when he was there but couldn't. It was a strange wrenching sensation, as if her heart were literally being wrung inside out, and then detail after detail, memory after memory suddenly reversed their significance and became, instead of irritating, unbearably poignant. Like that perennially clutched, infuriatingly produced timetable which she realized now Jason had simply *needed* to cling to, even in his sleep. Or that annoying habit of following her around, dogging her every footstep, desperate for her goodwill when it *must* have been clear, yes surely it had been clear to him, that all she felt for him was exasperation, even at times downright enmity. But where else had he to go, poor thing? Not to little Googie, cheerful and good-natured as she was, not to dark distant Doris, not to a father so quick (from Jason's point of view) to turn against him. But worst of all was the memory of him on that last rainy morning, standing so brave and neat and painstakingly put together in the madras jacket and water-slicked black hair—why was this so much more painful than if he had been his usual adolescent mess?—waiting obediently to step off into the dark void until his mother kept him safe again. Why, he was so young to be so alone. Only a baby! Googie was only seven years younger. And *she*, a grown woman, a surrogate mother on whom he depended for so much and from whom he'd asked so damn little, hadn't even bothered to kiss him good-bye!

"We even missed our anniversary," Arthur said.

"What?"

"The fifteenth of June," Arthur said, "except who could remember anything but that he was leaving on the *sixteenth*? Oh nuts. Our tenth anniversary. And I was going to do something wonderful about it too."

"Oh, well," Janet said.

"What do you mean, 'oh well'?"

But the discussion of dates had already sent her to consult the tidal chart/calendar, souvenir of Nickerson's Hardware, missing on that fateful day of Jason's defection but now retrieved and hung by its string on a knob of one of the white kitchen cupboards. "Yes, that's right," Janet said, turning around. "It *is* tomorrow that he's going to Switzerland. Oh, do let's call him, darling, say bon voyage or something, not let him go off with that sour taste in all our mouths."

"I did call him. He's not leaving tomorrow," Arthur said. "Don't you want to get your suit on?"

"What do you *mean* not leaving tomorrow?" Janet said, though more aghast at the fact that transparent, tenderhearted Arthur, who told all and needed to have everything else patiently explained to him, should have remembered the date of Jason's departure and never even mentioned it. What else was Arthur remembering that he wasn't mentioning?

"It was a mistake," Arthur said. "They made a mistake about the date."

"*Mistake?*" Janet said. "There was no mistake. Don't you realize that they—"

"—deliberately tricked me and cheated me as if I were a common thief," Arthur said. "Yes . . . but damn it, I didn't mean him any harm. I love him. I'm his father."

"Oh, Arthur—Arthur, dear."

"Leave me alone, damn you," Arthur said, burying his wet face in the crook of his elbow. "I've done my best for him. I can't do any more. I'm through."

"Now, Arthur, you musn't—"

"Leave me alone!"

She did not allow herself to rise to the provocation, which was a kindness, and instead let him cry it out in peace, which she hoped was a mercy. Nevertheless, watching Arthur sob his heart out into the cold white formica, head encompassed by his arms like a child at rest time, she couldn't help wondering why the man insisted on taking it so hard. After all, *had* Arthur done his best for his son? Not really. Had either of them? Of course not. And how would they ever succeed in disentangling themselves from the ghastly humiliation of it all if they insisted they had done their best and it was their best that had been rejected? Whatever the cost, she must make this point clear to Arthur, Janet thought, watching over him patiently until he had dried his eyes with a back-pocket handkerchief and blown his nose with a trumpeting sound, the usual signal that he had now passed over into the realm of action.

"Arthur," Janet said. "You're taking it too hard."

"Thank you."

"Oh, darling, please, be reasonable. What's really so shocking or unexpected about what happened today if you view it in the light of previous developments?"

"Damn it, I did my best," Arthur said. "I've always tried, with everything I had, to—"

"But *have* you done your best? Have I? You *know* that we haven't . . . Arthur, don't glare. If we don't put this whole wretched lie in its proper perspective, what will we have understood?"

"Wait a minute," Arthur said, getting up to fetch himself a bottle of beer from the refrigerator in the kitchen area. He offered a swig to Janet, who smiled and refused, and sat down again, smoothing back a long strand of his straight black hair which immediately fell over his ear again, as it always did under stress. "—*what* are we supposed to have understood?"

"Well, consider it from his angle, darling—sweetheart, don't look as if I'm killing you, it's insulting to both of us—well, here we are with our own lives, merry and gay, with an adorable child, doing as we please, a self-contained, natural unit. Jason doesn't belong in it, we don't even try to make him think he belongs in it, and why should we? It would be a lie basically."

"If you're trying to tell me I've been a rotten father to him, I know that," Arthur said, his eyes filling with tears.

"Darling, that's irrelevant to what I've been saying. . . . Now, where was I? Oh, yes, there we are, a self-contained, natural unit. Admit it, we hardly even think of him when he's not around, or even cancel a date for his sake. You've never even taken him on a trip by yourself, Arthur, or camped with him, or cooked for him, the way Bob did for that awful Tom, or Seymour does with that snotty-nosed Buddy. *I'm* the only one who's ever cooked for him, actually, or taken him on a trip by himself for that matter. To see my sister in Philadelphia before Googie was born. Remember? Though I must say it wasn't so cute when *your* sister said afterwards, 'You want to hear something adorable? Jason asked Claire why you weren't nice to him the way she is, and Claire explained it was because you didn't have any children.'"

"What does my *sister* have to do with it?"

Plenty, though that was another whole subject. So was Arthur's elderly mother, who thank god lived in New York. "All I'm trying to point out, darling, is how different this is from our feeling about Googie, who literally dominates our lives. But that's the whole spiritual point of having children of your own, isn't it?" ("He is my own," Arthur said.) "That at first you think, my god, I'll never have a free moment again—oh, you've no idea how desolate I used to feel when you went off to class and I sat bound to that tiny creature in its crib, or wandered up and down endlessly, aimlessly, pushing my stroller in wind, snow, ice and rain, reduced to seeking conversation with Shirley Kane or Betty Carlsbad. And then one day, suddenly—I remember exactly when it happened, you were in Washington for a long weekend—suddenly you realize that it's a kind of quintessential responsibility. That you're a *parent*." Janet leaned forward, putting her hand over Arthur's, who childishly lifted his beer bottle with the other. "Arthur, I know he's your own. But confess it. We've never felt quintessentially responsible for Jason. He's volunteer work on our part, and how could it be otherwise? But, don't you see, meanwhile, he's building up a life of his own, a life he has to abandon every time we whistle and come running? Naturally, he resents it, how could he not? *We're* the ones who thought it would be such a great treat for him up here, not him. So one day, he goes to his Mommy and says—funny how he still calls her Mommy— 'Mommy, I don't *want* to go away for a whole month.' So she says, 'All right, look, we'll clip off a week at the beginning, a week at the end, no one will be the wiser' . . . You see?"

"Helping him lie, cheat, scheme, to get away from his own father."

"Arthur, I just *explained* how it was."

"I know how it was," Arthur said. "I just can't be so sanguine about it."

"I'm not sanguine," Janet said, "I'm far from sanguine, I assure you. I regard the circumstances as tragic. But I still don't see what we'll accomplish keeping ourselves fixated on how he's wronged us, when in fact his behavior has been au fond entirely natural and normal under the circumstances."

"Don't you think I know I've failed him as a father?" Arthur said. "Don't you think I realize how . . . ?"

The conversation ended a few sentences later. Arthur was simply unable or, worse, unwilling to see that the truth examined dispassionately was far less dramatic and terrible than these obsessions with which he insisted on torturing himself. But then Arthur often mistook the truth, especially from her mouth, as a weapon rather than as a cool illumination in whose aura they could bask as in a pale late afternoon sun. (As in the case of a few overenthusiastic girl PhD candidates, who Arthur refused to believe were not interested in the principles of sociology alone.) The two of them parted, neither having risen to the quarrel that hung in the air, though still ogling the bait, and, avoiding any further mention of the beach, spent a coldly cordial rest of the day sidestepping each other—Arthur with exaggerated politeness, always a danger sign, as if Janet were a former ally who had defected and therefore a worse enemy than if she had been a stranger all along. But I'm *not* an enemy, and I'm certainly no stranger, Janet told herself that evening after dinner when Doris, who was still in a benign frame of mind, had fed Googie and put her to bed, and she and Arthur sat far apart on the thin foam rubber couch, strung together on the same taut wire, staring into a nervous modernistic fire. No, hardly a stranger. Then why did he always insist on treating her like one, especially when all she was trying to do was bring a few home truths to his attention? She picked up her martini grumpily, and looked over at Arthur who was grumpily picking up his, suddenly seeing him like a creature through the wrong end of the telescope: dazzlingly bright, clear in all his particulars, but tiny, minute, the incredible shrinking man. He was actually in the middle of a long story, which he was telling to the fire and occasionally to her, all about the famous summer when he was finishing up his dissertation at Columbia and met Claire at a party on Claremont Avenue. He still wasn't quite sure what she was doing there, because she wasn't a graduate student. No, even in those days, Claire was much too coolly amused by the scene, too sophisticated and detached for any kind of serious academic work. Extraordinarily forthright too. Even in the taxi going back to her apartment on Perry Street, she had told him plainly that she was madly in love with an English actor whom she intended to marry as soon as she got him away from his wife. Arthur had guessed that she probably would. In fact, after he and Claire were divorced, he had automatically guessed so again. But no, though she and the actor stayed in touch, Claire had preferred to remain the mistress of her own affairs—Arthur chuckled to himself professorially at the unintentional pun. Yes, really, when he thought about it, and whatever else you wanted to say about her, she was really an extraordinarily independent woman. And there still weren't many of those around, even these days with all the crap about fem lib. She hadn't even ever asked for alimony, only child support. Of course her parents were rich, the father a stockbroker. That made a difference.

"Actually," Arthur said, "I've never been sure why she married me in the first place." No? "But she was absolutely determined to go through with it even though we both knew it would be an absolute disaster from the start. At the end of the ceremony, I even kissed her mother by mistake. Handsome woman—she always wanted me to keep in touch. And even she used to admit that nobody could do anything with Claire, she was so willful and headstrong. Beautiful too, and she knew it, which was probably the reason." He turned to Janet with an interested, puzzled look, like an eager boy with a question. "She used to wear her hair differently. Not cropped the way you do, but sort of all gold and ringlety and piled up on top, so that we used to call her Little Aphrodite. You know what I mean? Also, the clothes were different then too, of course. And Claire did love clothes. She used to be especially fond of these sheer sort of fluttery dresses—chiffon, is that it?—with little tiny buttons down the front, and all sorts of vivid colors. A kind of rosy red especially. She doesn't seem to wear much red these days, but at that time with that blond hair all piled up, it was really quite fetching. Bob Carlsbad had a thing about her, you know."

"Did he?"

"Why so angry suddenly?" Arthur said. "Why so distant?"

"Angry? Distant?" Janet said. "Yes, I suppose you might say so—a little."

"Why, because I was talking about Claire?"

"Well, after all, Arthur," Janet said, smiling tightly, "she's hardly of the same consuming interest to me as she seems to be to you."

"What are you talking about? Isn't she Jason's mother?"

"Yes, of course she interests me, as Jason's mother. But as your former wife—well, I'm afraid I just haven't achieved that degree of sophistication. In fact, I'm afraid it's all a bit embarrassing to me, this talk of former lovers, taste in clothes and so on."

"I'm hungry," Arthur said. "Are you hungry?"

"Starving. Just a minute, I'll heat us up some soup."

"I'll heat it up," Arthur said.

"It's okay, you made the martinis."

"*I'll* heat it up," Arthur repeated and, stepping over her feet, walked unsteadily over to the kitchen cupboard, where the tidal chart was hanging, and took out a can which he immediately began to jam up against the wall opener. Had he heated up cans for *her* too, or, in spite of the "amused detachment from the scene" (*ha, ha*) had she turned out to be one of those motherly types who never let a man do a thing around the house? Especially a man like Arthur, who had already gotten himself into trouble with the simplest kitchen task, somehow managing to let the top of the can sink down into its contents, and was now desperately trying to pry it up, first with a fork and then with the only decently sharp knife that had come with the house. My god, Janet thought, leaving the watery dregs of her martini and getting to her feet, married to me for ten long years—it was our anniversary—not to mention the two abortive years with the other one, and he still doesn't even know how to open a can of soup. One would think that with all that domestic experience under his belt a man would be able to do something around the house, not fumble around like a child. But then, in so many ways Arthur *was* a child, as much as Googie, or that son of his. "Oh, give that to me," Janet said. "What's the matter with you?" Arthur said, grabbing the can back and sloshing its juices over both of them. "I'm accomplishing it. Give a man a chance."

"Oh, stop arguing," Janet said.

"Hey, who the hell do you think you *are*, talking to me like that?" Arthur said. "Who the hell do you think *I* am?"

"The point," Janet said, closing her eyes wearily, and opening them up again after a deep sigh, "the point, my dear Arthur, is not always who anybody is, though the matter seems to fascinate you endlessly. The point at the moment is merely this can of soup, and that you are unable to open it. Now, if you would kindly—" But Arthur had already left it for her in a puddle on the stainless steel sink and had gone back to sit on the sofa. She pried the lid out with a fingernail, bruising the little hump of soft skin underneath, and plopped the stuff from the can—onion soup—into the nearest saucepan. "Do you want an omelette too?" Janet asked over her shoulder. "Or will this be enough?"

"I don't want anything," Arthur said, staring dismally into the fire.

"Oh, Arthur, don't be a baby. You said you were hungry."

"I don't want anything," Arthur said, getting up to leave the room by way of the night on the outside deck. "Forget it."

Okay, fine, Janet thought. Let Arthur's appetite be his own business for a change. (Ho, ho—and how would the mother and sister like *that*?) If he got hungry later on, he could fix himself something to eat like any other normal human being. Personally, she herself was starving. She took the soup impatiently off the fire before it had even come to a boil, poured some into a mug, Arthur's favorite, the red one with the rooster on it, she noticed guiltily after she had stuck a spoon in, and then put it on a saucer, adding a few soda crackers on the side, and brought the whole thing over to the fire. Looking around almost furtively, she removed the old *Saturday Evening Post* from the bottom shelf of the coffee table where she had stuck it away the day Jason left, and began to spoon up her soup and leaf through its pages with a kind of schoolgirlish pleasure. Such a wonderfully reassuring and peaceful feeling, her first of the summer, almost reminiscent of when she was a little girl, cozily sick in bed with the flu, and her sister, the one who had been so nice to Jason that time, would come home from school, bringing in the fresh cold air from outside, and magazines like the *Ladies' Home Journal* for her to leaf through, and colored hard candies to suck on. She set aside the soup for a moment, and began to read an article about a fire in a Catholic orphanage in Ohio. A silly story, she supposed, and written in the usual absurdly slick style, but fascinating nevertheless. Nuns hoisting their habits and climbing into fiery windows, which, say what one would about the Catholic Church, required enormous courage. The efforts of the small local hospital to round up enough plasma to treat the children. The suffering of the burned children themselves. Pictures of the results of the plastic surgery two years later. The spoon rattled in the mug. She looked up reluctantly.

"Goddamn it," Arthur said. "What did you mean talking to me like that before?"

"Oh, Arthur, please."

"What do you mean, oh, Arthur, please? Since when have I begun to bore your ladyship?"

"Arthur, control yourself. Here, sit down. If you're hungry I'll get you some soup."

"I don't want to control myself. I don't want your goddamn soup either," Arthur said, weaving somewhat, as the writers and poets did at faculty parties after their readings at Gorham. "I want to know what was the meaning of that attack before."

"What attack? No one attacked you."

"Oh, didn't they? Snatching that can from me with those eyes full of hate. What sin against reason have I committed this time?"

"There was no sin, Arthur," Janet said, attempting to engross herself in the *Saturday Evening Post* once more, "and I am not going to go on with this stupid discussion. If you want to go on with this stupid discussion I'm afraid you'll have to do it all by yourself."

"Oh, great. So now I'm supposed to talk to myself. In my own house—or am I mistaken in assuming that this is my house and I pay the rent here?"

"Yes, this time you do pay the rent, and all our other living expenses," Janet said, eyes downward, leafing briskly through pages. "Okay? Now, do you suppose that for once you could keep quiet? I am simply not interested in having an argument at this moment."

"What do you mean, this time?"

"Oh, Arthur, for god's sake. Shut up."

"Shut *up*? Shut *up*?" Arthur cried. "Who the hell do you think you *are* that you can talk to me like that? Who the hell do you think *I* am?"

"Arthur," Janet said, pushing the silly magazine aside once and for all, "the issue is not who either of us *is*. The issue is that I am trying to have a quiet mug of soup, and that as usual I can't. Now stop it, just stop it. There wouldn't even be a quarrel now if not for you." In the dark back of the house, a child cried. Googie.

"So now it's all *my* fault," Arthur said.

"Yes, it *is* your fault," Janet cried, with tears of exasperation. "It's all your fault. It's always your fault. Now, *get off my back*! I'm not your poor son!"

Arthur obediently kept quiet. Only, quieter than she had bargained for, and for longer than she could bear. He merely looked down at her stunned, the straight black lock of hair hanging over one ear as usual, mouth slack, adenoidal, as if he were waiting to suck back the breath she had just knocked out of him. She looked back at him appalled. Oh, god, it's Jason's fault, Janet thought, hurriedly, yes, Jason's. . . . But *why* had he wanted to rob her of her husband, her home, her happiness, her summer?

When the Wind Blew

IT WAS JUNE OF 1952, a beautiful Paris afternoon. Leaves fluttered on the Boulevard St. Germain, and shabbily elegant Parisians strolled in the dappled sunlight underneath, the men pinched and thin like scholars, the ladies in wide-shouldered suits and clog-like shoes, with an occasional amazing outburst of prewar silver fox cape or jacket. And I, in my fuzzy pink sweater and ponytail, sat outside the Deux Magots with Norman, having a Cinzano and trying to fix it all in my mind against the day when I had to go home again. True that the day was still far off, in September, and true that we had just come back from picking up our mail at the American Express, which always made it worse, especially when read waiting for the bus in front of the Opéra, and conscious of that incredibly baroque and beautiful vision of itself looming behind. And not that my mail was anything worse than usual: just a note from my parents with a single nylon stocking enclosed, though sometimes it could be a wad of toilet paper folded flat, an American five-dollar bill, another stocking—they had this peculiar determination to outwit French Customs—also an aerogram from a former Southern boyfriend named Randolph saying he was now in analysis, and how *was* I? I stuck them away in my filet, next to the Paris *Tribune*, and took out the graph-paper cahier in which I had lately been trying to make notes against future nostalgia. "L'Opéra. Façade. Every vertical line has a draped statue perched on top of it. At the sides all the globes and flutings and horizontals and verticals swoop in and out and tear apart from each other until all you can do is laugh. . . ." Why laugh? From every point of view, emotional, former English major at Gorham, it made no sense, and I instinctively turned to Norman for a bit of consolation, something along the order of after Proust and Flaubert, etc. how could *I* possibly hope to describe the beauties of Paris?—which was the kind of consolation that Norman could be very good at. But he had this Basque beret shoved deep down on his forehead, always a sign of intense intellectual preoccupation, and totally oblivious of the passing scene, and even probably of sitting at a sidewalk café at all, which had never meant anything to him in the first place, sipped his Perrier, deeply absorbed in his own mail, a letter from Erika Hauptmann announcing she was on her way to some cultural congress in Frankfurt and stopping off first in Paris to see an old friend. It was the time of year when people were always announcing that they were coming to Paris and expecting you to be thrilled about it, new graduates, old professors, friends of parents, girlfriends who had just got married, and Erika's letter was in the same category, only a note, really, on *Île de France* stationery, the kind of thing that passengers going on to Le Havre send off at Southampton when they've already packed and have nothing more to do, though Norman took it very seriously and read it through several more times before he finally stuck it away in the pocket of his polo shirt.

"I simply don't see how she can face going back to Germany, can you?" I said.

"She's German."

"She's a German *Jew*," I said, turning around.

"Oh, Sonia, Sonia," Norman said, shaking his head over me and repeating my name as usual, which for dark Dostoievskian reasons he liked, though I was actually fair. "Intellectuals from all over the *world* will be there—Silone, Koestler, Moravia, Camus—"

I think he also added Nabokov (Nicholas), and probably Sidney Hook. Then, shaking his head again, he opened his copy of *Les Temps*

Modernes and flicked over a page with a moistened thumb, or maybe that day he just buried himself in *La Condition Ouvrière,* I forget which—he was very hot on Simone Weil at the time, so probably it was *La Condition Ouvrière.* Anyway, what was the point in persisting? There were people who thought and people who felt. And I? I supposed I was one who thought about feeling—which was why, maybe, that *CGT* envelope sticking out of the pocket of Norman's polo shirt kept piquing me with something like jealousy. Not actual jealousy. No young girl who had ever studied with Erika Hauptmann for an entire semester, even more terrified by those wiry gray-black curls, high haunches and long juicy teeth than by the subject, which was totalitarianism, wondering why she had turned out to be so lousy at philosophy when she had always thought she would be so good at it, could ever be piqued by actual jealousy. Still, the fact remained that Erika Hauptmann had written to Norman, and not to me, though we had both taken her famous seminar together, and though, now that I thought of it, Erika had given me an A and Norman only a B. Not that high marks and accademic honors signified intellectual distinction. Far from it, as Norman often pointed out, and I agreed. Also, Erika— why was it so hard for me to call her by her first name, when Norman did it so easily?—Erika hardly made any great secret of her feeling that teaching mere girls was a waste of her time, which was why the seminar was also open to deserving boys from nearby colleges, and Norman was certainly deserving, a poor boy from Springfield, working his way through Amherst on the G.I. Bill, and grateful for every word. I could still remember him vividly across the long seminar table, nodding with excitement as Erika made dark dire predictions on the state of the world in her dark dire German accent, unable to keep himself from interjecting enthusiastically at intervals "—and not only *that,* but *also*—!" There was also some awed couple named Schulz, from Idaho, who had evidently never seen a refugee before and went around taking everything down on a tape recorder. But then, Norman and I weren't in love in Gorham. In fact we hadn't even fallen in love in tourist class, also of the *Île de France,* where by coincidence we found ourselves sailing together last June, but on the boat train pulling out of Le Havre, when, seated across from him, I suddenly realized how beautiful Norman was, with those pouting sullen red lips and thick black sooty eyelashes, and curly Jewish curls. Not like my Aunt Rose's Stanley at all, who was also considered almost too pretty for a boy— but deeply sensual, though he didn't realize it, boyishly, charmingly, insistingly demanding, like Chéri almost—if I had pearls. . . .

Oh, god, yes, I'm in *Paris*, I thought, looking around and wondering again how I would ever get myself to leave the place, *Paris*. And then Morty and Elaine Cohen strolled by, smiled, and consented to sit down when waved to, and it was all Hemingway again: Métro kiosks plastered round with colored notices and posters, fluttering leafy boulevard, the little saucers under our apéritifs with the old francs still imprinted on them, the Cohens looking exactly like the genuine expatriates they were. Especially Morty Cohen, elegantly bald with long sideburns, and the look authentic, of having studied brilliantly with F. O. Matthiessen at Harvard, and then chucked it all immediately after the war to come to Paris. They even had their own apartment on the rue de Verneuil, with a fat concièrge in a blue smock downstairs, and five flights up, after a race with those self-extinguishing minuteries that went black a few seconds too soon, a little girl in pink feet pajamas who looked like a Renoir and spoke only French, and a bonne à tout faire addressed as "Madame" who looked after her and often made us impecunious Americans a gigot on Sundays. In fact, with all their savoir-faire the Cohens were amazingly kind to visiting compatriots and had been very generous to Norman and me with tips about the best place to change money on the black market, where to look for cheap hotel rooms when we outgrew the Cité Universitaire. Or rather when *I* outgrew it, Norman being as usual almost Talmudically indifferent to his surroundings, a quality of mind I admired except when I thought of myself as downstairs minding the store. Though it wasn't Morty Cohen at all, but *I* who finally happened on our marvelous hotel on the rue de la Harpe, a tiny obscure Arab street, with incredibly romantic adjoining rooms, each with long maroon-velvet portières, and a dim rose-colored light in the ceiling that went off when you switched on the dim rose-colored light over the bed, and also a tiny balcony where, by standing on tip-toe, you could see a slice of traffic on the Boulevard St. Michel directed by a gendarme with cape and whistle. Actually, the Hôtel de la Harpe had turned out to be a maison d'assignation, which explained all the mysterious vacuuming and changing of sheets at odd hours, but I was rather proud of that too. I didn't even mind when Morty Cohen teased me about it. I only minded when he kept smiling and said "—*two* rooms?" Because of course Norman's morality had nothing to do with it, only the question of needing separate privacies for thinking and work. Unfortunately, those rose-colored lights drove Norman crazy, he was always squinting under them, sneaking off to the hardware store for clear bulbs with strong wattage, making shade-like contraptions of paper clips and typing paper, which the patron invariably got the chambermaid to take down, and who was always giving us peculiar looks when we came home together anyway, so that I always wanted to stop and explain about the work and the privacy. Not even explain—apologize.

"Eh, bien, mes vieux, ça va?" Morty Cohen said, smiling at us, and then ordering from a hovering waiter a Punt e Mes for himself and a citron pressé for Elaine, which immediately made my Cinzano a tourist drink advertised by every ashtray on every café table.

"Oh si, bien sûr, ça va Morty," I said, though Norman merely looked up and nodded, slitting an overlooked unslit page with the picture postcard of the Tour Eiffel that I had been about to send to Aunt Rose, and spritzing some of the soda for Elaine's citron pressé into his empty Perrier glass after asking if she minded if he took some of her seltzer. He could certainly have been a little bit more cordial and impressed, especially since the Cohens were Norman's contact to begin with, through a mutual friend on the *Carleton Miscellany*, and that after all, even the name Cohen was practically straight out of *The Sun Also Rises*. But the fact of their genuine expatriatism had never meant anything to him—"Okay, Sonia, suppose you tell *me* why you have to live in Paris to write a novel about your mother in the Bronx," though Morty had spoken many times of aesthetic distance—and neither did the fact that Morty truly spoke French like a native, or at least a native of Normandy, which was what some Frenchmen took him for, it had something to do with certain vowels. Whereas, the best *I* had ever done was be mistaken for a Swede, and that was at a Fulbright reception. But then Norman had a way of dismissing so many things as intellectually unserious, like my being in France on a Fulbright, for example, instead of a G.I. Bill like him, and could even make the extra stipend seem frivolous—which wasn't too hard with all those skinny impoverished Parisians walking around, and in an era when poverty was still assumed to be instructive. Also, Norman was one of those people who thought even the French were being affected when they spoke French with a French accent, and was a multiple "oui"er besides, like a multiple sneezer, who said "oui, oui, oui" quickly to every question to get it over with, instead of one "oui" at a time, which might have prolonged the conversation.

A skinny wizened old gentleman stopped by to talk to Morty, a French friend of theirs whom we had met the night before when we were having dinner with the Cohens on a red velvet banquette at the Brasserie Lipp, and as Morty commenced the answer to a question with an ". . . alors, comment dirai-je?" accent perfect, hand motions correct, palms turned down, a slight Gallic shift of the shoulders, and Elaine looked on eagerly, pointy breasted and smiling, reminding me again that after all these were people who knew Eugene Jolas, who had known Joyce, beauties who were having a "succès fou" in society that season, heiresses who slashed their wrists, a man named Kaplan who seemed to be some subterranean intellectual force—who should come squeezing through past several tables on the other side but little Bobby Simmons, smiling like a nervous sweaty chipmunk and saying, "Do you mind?" a question it was already too late to answer. Then Johnny Peters stopped out on the sidewalk when he saw us, laughing with his black Sambo teeth, and dragging along Marie-Claire Gauthier, who looked even glummer than usual in her thin sweater and cheap cotton dress with the belt that dangled drearily down her middle like a wilted phallus. This time, Norman put down his *Condition Ouvrière* and shook hands with amazingly brisk seriousness and respect, in sptie of Marie-Claire's being such a violent Communist and himself such an anti-Communist—though not violent, since in Erika's course the Soviet Union tended to drift in and out of being totalitarian, like the sun through dark clouds. Was he impressed that Marie-Claire also took the condition of the workers so seriously, or was it only that she *looked* like Simone Weil?

"How's your project?" little Bobby said to me, like a fellow con-spirator, ". . . marching?"

"Sure. How's yours?"

"Marching."

Since we were both lying, we dropped the subject quickly. Bobby was no great talker anyway, on account of being a musician and also something of a stammerer. He kept looking around furtively at all the café tables as if his mother had just stepped out and he was trying to get it all in before she came back. But guilt about the extra stipends aside, there *was* something about our Fulbrights that always did go amok. I dont' remember Bobby's project, but my own, which had looked great on a State Department application in triplicate and which I tried not even to think about anymore, was *supposed* to have been a study of American expatriate writers after World War II. Only, there *weren't* any, except maybe Richard Wright, and Julian Green—and I guess Morty Cohen, if he ever finished his novel. Then, there was the case of Kenny Schwartz, who had been sent down to Aix-en-Provence to do a study of the influence of *Uncle Tom's Cabin* on French litera-ture, and even some guy in Rome who'd spent his entire grant on a rosticceria, which to make it even more embarrassing, he was operat-ing at an enormous profit. Johnny Peters had burst out laughing, and was telling us about this friend of his who had been arrested on his very first day in Paris because the flics thought he was an Arab, when Morty's old French gentleman turned around to me unexpectedly.

"Et vous deux," he said, "vous avez bien diné hier soir?"

"Ah, *oui*, monsieur, *j'adore* le choucroûte," I said, which the Brasserie Lipp happened to be famous for, and trying to keep calm though I was terribly excited to be addressed by a real Frenchman. I nudged Norman.

"Oui, oui, oui," Norman said, briefly interrupting his point to Marie-Claire à propos Johnny's story, that the French also had a lot to answer for in terms of colonial exploitation.

The old gentleman looked at me icily before turning back to an enthralled Elaine. "Mademoiselle," he said, "ici nous parlons le langage de Descartes, mais si vous voulez le reviser, allez-y."

Revise the French language? What had I done? I looked at Morty in a panic and suddenly saw the plat du jour printed clearly on the menu of the Lipp: "Choucroûte garnie." I had mistaken the gender of sauerkraut. I wished I could say, en passant as it were, and with a casual ça alors shrug that "chez nous" we spoke "le langage de Shak-spère," only we were a hell of a lot politer to strangers, except that I couldn't trust my French to come out even by the end of the sentence. Anyway, that white-haired emaciated Gallic version of Leonard Lyons had already kissed Elaine's hand and gone on to bend over another enthralled group at another café table out on the sidewalk.

Morty Cohen was highly amused. "Ma chère, that was Paul Guil-lotine." Guillotine? Evidently I hadn't caught the name. "A runner-up for the Prix Goncourt last year," Morty Cohen said, still amused, still good-humored, but head now a bit cocked, air a bit chiding.

"I'm sorry, Morty, but I don't think literary achievement has any-thing to do with it," I said, scrupulously trying to avoid any ad homi-nem references. "It's a question of simple courtesy. I mean I *expect* to be insulted by the French bourgeoisie, I'm almost used to it by now—" Bobby started to disagree, but couldn't get it out fast enough. He was crazy about his landlady out near the Bois de Boulogne. "—but when even a famous novelist—"

"He's also a famous Socialist," Norman said, with that exasperating knack of knowing facts about what he couldn't even bother to pro-nounce.

"Le langage de Descartes . . . choucroûte, donc je suis," I said to Morty, who laughed but in a very controlled Jamesian way.

"I mean, not only a novelist, but a *Socialist*, mind you," I said to Johnny Peters, "—chou-croûte, don't bother me." Johnny guffawed, but Johnny was always good for a laugh, so there was no satisfaction in it.

"Well," Norman said, "I like France, but I've never liked the French." Not too unexpectedly Marie-Claire nodded glumly before she launched off on her counter retort, which was about the Peek-skill riots and the use of germ warfare in Korea, using the word "noir," which shocked me but didn't seem to bother Johnny.

I looked out across the Boulevard St. Germain, suddenly aching with loneliness, thinking how cut off from its life we were by being stuck together under the awning of the Deux Magots, and all foreign-ers, even Marie-Claire, who by sticking around so closely to attack us was a foreigner too, and how the sudden glistening black rain had made everything painfully, glisteningly beautiful. When I came to again, Johnny and Morty were discussing *The Ambassadors*, the part where Strether sees Chad eating an omelette aux fines herbes with Mme. de Vionnet and understands, Johnny being an even more elegant stylist than Morty, in spite of the big gleaming white teeth and small dark shiny face and the bulgy yellow eyes with red veins in them. He had just sent off a long analysis of *The Sound and the Fury* to the *Kenyon Review*, with a good chance of having it accepted. By then Marie-Claire was telling Elaine, who supported Morty by working as a secretary at the U.S. Embassy, how she had once blasphemed by drinking a Coca-Cola on top of the Milan Cathedral. Elaine nodded eagerly, as she did to anybody French, though she knew very well we *never* ordered cokes, only, in the soft-drink department, citron pressé and maybe soda d'orange, which Morty had learned to drink in North Africa and told us about. "Am-me-mericans are so ad-do-lescent," Bobby Simmons said, all nervous and sweaty again, looking around furtively. Out on the sidewalk, that skinny mean old bird, Monsieur Guillotine, continued his gossip column rounds, avoiding the outer rim of American tourists at their café tables as if they were soiled.

"I mean, can you imagine *sleeping* with that man?" I said to Elaine.

"Mind your own business," Elaine said, laughing, which made me look around at her sharply. She was full of surprises, this girl, not least a gorgeous sexy body to go with her harlequin glasses and homely secretary's face, and all kinds of good-natured dirty stories, like how she had made Morty kneel down and shave off the top of her pubic hair the first time she wore a bikini. Norman got up, signaling me with an inclination of the head, and telling the group that we were meeting Erika Hauptmann at the boat train tomorrow, which was the first I heard that we were going to meet her.

"*Erika Hauptmann?*" Morty said, suitably impressed, or perhaps more than suitably because the whole point about Erika was that she *wasn't* well known.

"Really?" Bobby said, and Elaine just kept looking kind of alert and eager and worried in Morty's direction on account of having missed a possible reference to a literary celebrity.

"What's the occasion?" Morty said.

"The Cultural Congress in Frankfurt."

"Ah, yes," Morty said.

"I can't imagine *how* she can bring herself to go back to Germany, can you?" I said to Morty, who smiled and shrugged.

"Oh, Sonia, Sonia," Norman said, sighing. Morty smiled and shrugged again. I wondered if Norman was ever going to get bald too, one day, though not elegantly bald like Morty, and also maybe fat. Then Norman gave Morty the money for his Perrier and I gave Norman the money to give Morty for my Cinzano, not counting the change, though there *had* been a few awkward incidents—there always were financially, dealing with Americans, including the time in Aix-en-Provence when Kenny Schwartz amazed us by inviting us to his house for dinner and told us laughingly afterwards that we had just eaten horse meat. "Ciao, baby," Johnny said, and I said "À bientôt."

Norman's G.I. Bill check wasn't due for a few days and so we stopped at a café and bought a few hard-boiled eggs from the wire basket next to the cash register, also a baguette, and a litre of wine that we put in my filet to eat upstairs in my room, where we always ate, though Norman's room was larger, but of course more cluttered with books and papers. Norman was still sore. We walked slowly back to the rue de la Harpe along a dark, glistening deserted quai, dark and glistening because it had been raining again, and then presently Norman sighed and stopped, sticking his palms behind him and hoisting himself up on the parapet, legs apart. I moved closer, and Norman put my hand between his legs. ". . . hey, I took her course too, you know," I whispered, omitting the part about the A. But though he went, "*hmm, hmm, hmm,*" and kept my hand gripped there by the strong steady pressure of his thighs, he turned his beautiful face away and looked off, as if he really didn't want to know what was going on, and so I looked off too, past his shoulder, where down below, on the other side of the Seine, fishermen fished by street-lamps.

As usual we were early, and of course the boat train was late. Worse, a whole lot of the American types we were always trying to avoid had already assembled around us, Harry Trumans with flowered sportshirts and cameras, kids from the mail basement of the American Express, plus a few of the usual skinny, shabby postwar Parisians, who kept giving us mean Yankee-Go-Home looks, and muttering about "les courants d'air," as if there had never been any drafts in France before we got there. I wondered why I didn't simply love France and hate the French, like Norman, but I could understand it about us being the spoilers, especially now, looking around in this beautiful chilly Gare St. Lazare with the leaded sooty fin de siècle skylight overhead, through which a few scant shafts of sunlight penetrated, making a cathedral of those of us waiting below. Over at another track, a long navy blue Grand Express Européen chuffed and idled in place, about to begin its long romantic journey to Bruxelles, Antwerp, Hook van Holland, Istanbul: destinations printed in gold on the outside of the voitures. There was even an old trainman portentously stooping to tap a steaming wheel, as in *Anna Karenina*. I saw red velvet seats inside and lace antimacassars and ladies in furs and muffs, a sommelier walking up and down between the fruit-laden tables in the wagon-restaurant, jingling his cups and chains of office.

"Oh, god, Norman," I said, gripping his arm, "it was *us* a year ago."

"You slept through Normandy," Norman said, shifting a skimpy bunch of red carnations from one hand to another, and wiping his sweaty palm on his tan corduroy pants in between. He had bought the flowers at a kiosk outside the métro, a decidedly uncharacteristic romantic gesture.

"It was the *wine*," I said, "it was overexcitement, not boredom."

"Flaubert country," Norman said, and I said, "I know," and let go of his arm. But then, Norman had always been anxious about trains, coming *and* going, and once at Brussels after a terrifically sexy romantic weekend, we had arrived at the station at six A.M., while they were still sweeping and hosing down the tracks, only to see what we took to be our train part in the middle and go off in different directions. Nevertheless, if he was this nervous now, what would he be like when Erika actually got here? I thought of her dreadful "little evenings" in her apartment over the garage in Gorham where we all sat around in a rigid semi-circle passing a plateful of Ritz crackers and pimento cheese while Erika, presiding in a black satin refugee dress that almost didn't make it over those high haunches, laid down the law on everything, sex, food, parents, stay away from, which we were all anxious to do anyhow, though her own mother seemed to have been the Saint of Königsberg. Maybe she would arrive with the Schulzes from Idaho and we would *all* have to follow her around with a tape recorder. I looked around again, and this time spotted a rather charming, stout, middle-aged woman standing nearby. By American standards not even attractive, but terrifically nice, even kind of sexy in a French way, dressed in a gray tailleur and furpiece, which was practically the uniform of a good parisienne in those days, and a velvet toque and veil, and considering the square torso, amazingly shapely legs in dark French stockings and black pumps. Actually, the more I looked, the more there did seem to be something special about her, not just her toque, which was unusual and obviously expensive, layer on layer of soft-colored velvet flower petals, or even her smile— I smiled back in surprise—which was certainly atypical in its good nature, though very French in that it revealed a gold tooth glinting in the back and was mainly directed at my handsome Norman. No, it was a certain je ne sais quoi, a combination of calme and volupté, the fact that under the dotted veil that covered her face and tied behind the toque, she wore a pair of square, rimless eyeglasses. She reminded me of a photograph I had once seen in *Le Figaro* of a young French bride in a white veil and also eyeglasses, of a line of confirmation girls stepping like little Mistinguetts through the portals of Chartres. "There, you *see*?" I wanted to say, pulling Norman by the arm, *"that's* it," and then I could imagine Morty smiling and saying, "You mean that je ne sais quoi?" and shut up. Anyway, it was too late. There was a sudden stiffening in the atmosphere. Then some fonctionnaire cried, *"Attention! Attention!"* and another somewhere down the line echoed, *". . . attention! . . . attention!"* and then the boat train came pounding into the station and screeched to a halt. By that point I wouldn't have been surprised if Erika had materialized like the damnation of Faust, another screech of wheels, billowing puffs of yellow smoke, then Erika smiling at us with her long juicy self-satisfied teeth. But in fact it was all very calm and quiet. The boat train settled down with an extra little push and shove and grind back and forth, and then just as everyone was wondering why the doors didn't open the doors unexpectedly opened, and the passengers gradually trickled out, and the trickle became a stream, and almost all of them stopped on the platform for a moment, looked around uncertainly, and then smiled and advanced, and people called people's names, and then Norman said, "There she is," and there she was, stopping uncertainly, frowning, smiling and advancing toward us.

"That's funny," I said.

"What's funny?"

"She looks so *American*."

"Don't be ridiculous."

But it was true. There we stood, Norman in his silly Basque beret pulled down low on his forehead, and I in my tight skirt and fuzzy pink sweater, whose neck had stretched during my stay abroad, and my heavy shoes with the plaid lining, looking, as we had thought, so very French, and there was Erika Hauptmann, the compleat European refugee in Gorham, striding toward us in a smart pale-tweed loose coat and a little navy-blue straw hat, brown alligator shoes with a handbag to match, and there we were again, Norman too, giving each other funny looks, as if we'd just failed the exam without even signing up for the course. However:

"*There* you are!" Erika cried, with a horribly familiar hoarse barking laugh that made my blood run cold—I won't attempt to reproduce her accent, first because it was inimitable, and secondly because in her case it owed as much to force of character as to circumstance—and held out her arms, prima donna style, not to us at all, but to that lovely French lady I had been admiring before and who, of all people, was evidently the friend Erika had come to Paris to see. Norman and I, silly eager smiles lost, stepped back and watched while the two women embraced, for so long and with such a *physical* need of each other, a quality that was totally atypical of Erika, that I was about to suggest to Norman that maybe we should take off, absent ourselves from their felicity a while, something like that, putting it on an intellectual basis to entice him, when Erika suddenly reached out from behind and caught him by the shoulder, keeping hold of her friend at the same time. Then she finally turned around and looked at the two of us and laughed that laugh again.

"Why, mon vieux!" she cried, still hanging on to her friend's hand, hers in a white cotton glove, the other lady's in black kid, "—how good to see you. . . . You too, little one."

"You remember Sonia," Norman said, and Erika again barked with laughter, though I wasn't sure what was so funny, the sight of me, the absurdity of the question, and introduced us to her friend, Madame Meyer (pronounced Meyère), whose hand we each shook gravely, telling her we were "enchanté."

"You look very French, little one," Erika said, looking me up and down thoughtfully, pausing with particular interest at my ponytail, "almost I would have taken you for a little French girl."

"Oh, she's become a complete Francophile," Norman said. "She even takes the Métro for pleasure."

"Actually, I once thought of being a French major at Gorham," I said, but Erika had already lost interest, and was looking around for the porteur, who at her first cry came running up, an emaciated old man in blue denim, sweating servilely and breathing hard under the amazingly large quantity of Erika's luggage, mostly brand new, valpacks and such, slung by a strap over his shoulder. (Norman and I, of course, had been so careful to bring shabby bags and travel light.) Then, while Norman tried too late and too hard to be helpful, and Mme. Meyer looked on, charming and amused, the poor old man raced us all out into the street and pushed and shoved and heaved us into an antique square green taxicab, right under the noses of a crowd of outraged, waiting French, who immediately began to mutter furiously, "Ô, ces Américains, alors—ces Américains!" A formidable woman, our professor. How in god's name had she managed it? Still, as we went bucking and honking through Paris traffic, with Erika pointing out various landmarks for our benefit, "Voyez, petits, la Madeleine . . . la Place de la Concorde . . ." patting Mme. Meyer's hand and telling her how glad she was to see her, ignoring poor Norman who was half-turned in his jump seat and staring with deepening gloom at his bouquet of red carnations, which somewhere along the line had been dumped in Mme. Meyer's lap, I thought that Erika was being kind of silly and pathetic also. Because what was the *point* of making such an issue of fending for herself, especially in Paris, especially when there was this beautiful young man dying to do it for her? The joke was that Erika was married, had been married twice, in fact, and being Erika had stuck the second wedding ring on top of the first, though actually she had very nice sweet clean little hands, like a surgeon's—the present husband being a likable mad invalid who sometimes wheeled himself out of the back bedroom during Erika's "little evenings" in the apartment over the garage, wheezed to us grandiloquently about some new kind of humanism he was going to spread throughout the universities, beginning, I think, with Wheaton College, and wheeled himself back again, otherwise staying pretty much out of the picture, especially since, as Erika had made a weighty public secret of, it was the husband's little streak of insanity that was the reason they had no children. A ludicrously obvious lie. It was impossible to imagine Erika with a child, except maybe eating it. I leaned forward and touched Norman consolingly on the shoulder, trying not to care when he looked at me as if he either couldn't place me for the moment or was surprised to find me in that taxi at all, and politely answered Mme. Meyer's polite questions about how was I enjoying Paris, and my studies and so on, thinking that oh, là, behind that dotted veil *here* was a lady who would have known how to languish. And then we crossed the Seine, circled behind the Chambre des Députés, and bounced and jounced down the cobblestones of the rue St. Jacques, and Erika announced that now, mes petits, we were on the Left Bank, and then we had stopped at her hotel.

Actually we knew the Hôtel des Saints-Pères perfectly well too, since it was one of the places Morty Cohen had advised us to look at the time of the Cité Universitaire, a modestly pretty little place, but awfully spare and clean, with a stringy-necked old bitch of a proprietress, probably a German left over from World War I, though she passed herself off as Alsatian, who all the time Erika filled out her police form and gave over her passport, kept glaring at Norman and me from behind her long polished mahogany counter, afraid we were going to steal her free copy of *Cette Semaine*, or leave fingermarks on the glass display case of perfumes and kid gloves. A valet de chambre in a striped apron came out to haul up Erika's luggage, and with Erika in the lead, and Norman just behind making ineffectual hand movements, we followed him upstairs, puffing and chugging up what seemed like ten flights, until we finally came to Erika's room, which was so dark and meager and redolent of a headachy lemon polish, that each of us, including the valet de chambre, went straight to the window as soon as we came in, looking up at a slice of blue Paris sky, and then down at an oblique corner of stone courtyard with a pot of red geraniums set against the wall. Still, I must admit that as Erika went around saying "Merveilleux!" to everything, creaky old armoire, narrow monk's bed, and even gave a terrifically approving nod to the bidet beside the sink—it wasn't Erika's enthusiasm I wondered about, but my own lack of it. Was there something in this immaculate grudging little room that escaped me? Something superior to our own maroon velvet portières and the rose-colored light in the ceiling that went off when you put on the one over the bed? Some exquisite point of Paris life that eluded me? Erika sank down on the one armchair, which looked more Danish modern than French, and I sat down on the hard narrow little bed—from the doorway, Norman gave me a dirty look, lèse majesté, preferring to stand with his bèret jammed into his pocket, like Raimu—and I smiled over toward the sink, where Mme. Meyer was filling an ironstone wash jug with water for the carnations.

"Ach, *kinder, kinder,*" Erika said, closing her eyes for a moment and taking a deep breath that she let out as a profound and passionate sigh. I looked at Mme. Meyer again, who smiled very gently, and very gently turned off the tap water, a gesture that reminded me of that long tender bereaved embrace at the Gare St. Lazare, and also suddenly of how my mother and my Aunt Rose had held each other when the news came from the nursing home that their father had died. Actually, they hadn't even liked the old man, and probably even hated him, but it didn't matter. "Ach, *kinder, kinder,*" Erika murmured again, and I wondered guiltily how I could have forgotten how much she had been through, how much it had cost her to come to this moment. She was even getting her old messed-up look back, of a kind of triumphant female impersonator.

"—*Enfin!*" Erika said, reviving and slapping the arms of her chair. "So, tell me, petite, what do you do with yourself here?"

"Me?" I said, looking over at Norman. Me. "Oh, well, nothing that it makes sense to tell actually. I mean I walk around a lot and try to engrave these impressions on my mind against future nostalgia, but—"

"But what?"

"Well, I mean technically I'm enrolled at the cours pour les étrangers at the Sorbonne, but—"

"Oh, là," Erika said, laughing in Mme. Meyer's direction.

"D'accord," I said, rather haughtily, "but it happens to be one of the terms of my grant."

"Never mind that," Erika said. "Stay away from courses."

"Really?"

"Of course. At your age what should matter but being in Paris?" She closed her eyes again briefly. "Nothing even *smells* in America. . . . Whom have you seen?"

I thought of Morty and Johnny and Bobby—and, laughing to make light of it, said Jean-Paul Sartre and Simone de Beauvoir, which was technically true, from across the room in a lovely little restaurant the Cohens had taken us to. They were having tiny red strawberries for dessert served on beautiful glossy green leaves, and Erika was right, the perfume had wafted clear across the room.

"Fraises des bois," Erika said. "How about Kaplan?"

"He's doing a series of articles on Indochina for *L'Express*," Norman said, "I'm meeting him when he comes back."

"Through whom?"

"Morty Cohen. He's a young novelist who lives here."

Erika shook her head. Pas connu, and how could he be since Morty wasn't published yet? Norman had just thrown in the novelist part to round out the sentence, as it were. Still, thank god he hadn't said Marie-Claire, also unknown, in this case an unpublished playwright, but a woman besides, and Erika had never taken kindly to the mention of other women intellectuals, which was why, I suddenly realized, the reference to Simone de Beauvoir had left her absolutely cold. It was funny, actually, to think of Erika playing deuxième sexe to anybody.

Suddenly she gave another one of those barking laughs that used to make us stop dreaming and sit up straight in the seminar. "—I'll give you a note," she said to Norman. "But tell me, is he still going ahead with his magazine, that idiot?"

"Who—Kaplan?" Norman said, shaking his head and laughing also. "I'm afraid so. My god, *what* an idiot."

"I don't like that," Erika said.

"Like what?"

"Who are you to impugn the intelligence of a man like Kaplan? You've never even met him."

"I wasn't impugning his intelligence," Norman said. "I regard him as a man of profound intelligence. I was merely taking up your point about the fact of a new magazine."

"And?"

"Well, I mean at a time like this—?"

"And can you tell me a better one? Believe me, these are dark hours for people like us. I've seen it all before."

No, you haven't, I thought, watching poor Norman get all red around the ears. Lay off him, you bitch. Anyway, she was wrong. Even in spite of Senator McCarthy, even with little Cohn and Schine crawling obscenely around our embassies and libraries, nothing, even Erika's dark pleasure in the possibility, could convince me that what had happened in Germany could also happen in the United States. I wondered if living in France and the shock of all those Yankee-Go-Home signs was turning me into some kind of superpatriot, and if in the fall I would be agreeing with all those statements and petitions signed by Diana Trilling and Irving Kristol. But no, what I felt was curiously not so much political as *personal*. It was like getting mad if anybody criticized Norman but me.

"Norman knows perfectly well these are dark hours for people like us," I said. "We just don't happen to think another little magazine is going to change anything," though I was afraid that the next time the subject came up, Norman would.

From the doorway, Norman smiled at me, a very bad sign in spite of his beautiful white teeth, since Norman rarely smiled except to suppress rage. His mother was the same way. The one time I had met her in the grocery in Springfield, she had smiled at me constantly, with tightly closed lips. I suddenly felt very depressed. Not that I had expected Norman to be grateful for my intervention, but still. . . .

"Does he always get so red around the ears?" Erika said to me amusedly, woman to woman, changing her tack. "—no, listen, Norman," she said, pointing a finger at him again, but briefly, a softer finger, more indulgent, "—écoute, mon chou, all Americans think every problem can be solved in two minutes. It's a national disease. You'll have to learn patience. Only, frankly, until you've met Kaplan—" another sudden spine-stiffening hoot of laughter. "—oh, Lotte, a Viennese creampuff! Every time he knows he's losing an argument, quick, down from the waist, *küss die hand.*"

Mme. Meyer smiled, putting the ironstone wash jug on the windowsill where it immediately became a vase of red carnations, and showed to lovely advantage. As it turned out, her hand had been kissed by Kaplan on many occasions, though not, quite obviously, on account of the loss of any heated arguments.

"Yes, that's right, you know him through Marcel Weber," Erika said. "How is he, after all these years?"

"Fine. He sends you regards."

"And Eric Mendlessohn? You see him too?"

"Of course. But now he's longing to see *you,*" and I could tell by Mme. Meyer's charming smile, and Erika's huge self-appreciative bark of laughter, that we had now stumbled into another libidinous mystery, like the two husbands. Then Erika wanted to know if Lotte remembered the time that Marcel, and Mme. Meyer did and wondered if Erika also remembered when, and Erika did, and soon they were deep in reminiscences of the past, a crowded chronicle of childhood friends, beloved family, brilliant professors at Heidelberg, immensely gifted musicians, supremely talented young writers and poets, and, oh yes, these marvelously clever political cabarets in Berlin—everything connected with Erika was always brilliant and superior and more so, starting with the sainted mother in Königsberg. Except, if those cabarets in Berlin were so clever politically and otherwise, how explain what happened afterward? But just about here I lost them anyway, because although they had both started out in English—Mme. Meyer's quaintly, lightly accented, almost Japanese, Erika practically Weber and Fields—they had inevitably lapsed into German, a language it still frightened me to hear, like the dialogue in war movies, and which I especially hated to hear Mme. Meyer speak. I couldn't follow it very well, anyway, except through the little bit of Yiddish my parents used to use when I was little and they didn't want me to understand. "Yiddish? That's only a low German dialect," Norman had once said, waving it off one time when we had first started going to bed together, and I had sat up and cried, "You got that from *her!*" and cried a lot more, and Norman was so bewildered he apologized. I mean, it just wasn't an intellectual subject.

Then we were in the midst of a deep silence, the deep fraught silence that a record makes when it's come to the end but is still scratchily going around. The two women were now just looking at each other, the one stiff and bolt-upright in her chair, the other caught in that half-light at the window with the carnations, like a Fragonard. This time Norman didn't need any nudging. We said good-bye, and they were very polite about saying good-bye back, but without any pretense of being sorry to see us go. As we left I understood Erika to say that she would now wash and unpack and make a few important phone calls, and Mme. Meyer reply in French that in any case she had to go back to her office for a while: evidently she was a clerk in some government bureau, another surprise, though it was still very hard times for everyone. We crossed the lobby with the old bitch patronne still glaring at us, and this vague feeling of disappointment at being done out of dinner, I, especially, on account of some stupid idea of wanting to show Erika how well I could eat fruit with a knife and fork.

Then outside it was Paris again. Across the street, a fat concièrge in a blue smock sat on a folding chair outside a building that was just like the Cohens' on the rue de Verneuil. Cabbage leaves clotted up the gutter. A little boy in skimpy pink shorts and sandals and a crocheted blue sweater with his elbows poking through, hopped up and down on one spindly leg, then the other. He was wearing brown sandals. I turned to Norman, wanting to say something like it would be all right, he'd see her again, only that would have been insulting. Anyhow, he was already jamming his beret down on his forehead and making what was for him an unusual suggestion, that why didn't we take a bus over to the Champs-Elysées and see an American movie? And so we did, and I couldn't help craning my neck to see the French subtitles.

Actually, we did see Erika again very soon, startlingly soon—I think the very next day when she called to cart us off to the Louvre—and also astonishingly often, considering we were only a pair of kids, former students after all, and she a prominent intellectual on her way to a cultural congress, and also busy renewing connections with such people as Jaspers in Basel, Heidegger in Bonn. ("Norman, wasn't Heidegger a Nazi or something?" "Oh, Sonia, Sonia," Norman said.) Though, of course, being Erika, she still had this idea that it was up to her to show us Paris, and so every time we met we always seemed to be riding around on the Seine on a bateau mouche, ducking under slimy bridges, windswept and freezing, marched through the Galerie D'Apollon at the Louvre—it was Mme. Meyer who finally and tentatively suggested the print room downstairs—listening to a girl student pianist in eyeglasses and a pink dress play Bach in the Salle Pleyel while she and Norman went "poum, poum, poum" under their breaths to keep up with the counterpoint, clinging to the narrow outside stairway on our way to the topmost ruined chapel of Ste. Chapelle, and once, on an all-day excursion to Chartres with Mme. Meyer along for the ride, being instructed in the art of the rosette window, each with a Guide Bleu in hand, Erika correcting it when it was mistaken. In fact, now that I think of it, Erika not only had a passion for churches but for Catholicism in general, a subject that like totalitarianism was also much in vogue at the time. (Funny to realize now how stylish she was, when in those days I always thought of her as a fearless forerunner.) But in fact, everything Catholic, and by extension, Christian, had a tremendous intellectual cachet for her, and one had only to say "six million" when she triumphantly dragged up Dietrich Bonhoeffer, or somebody like that, as if the hanging of one distinguished German theologian outweighed all those anonymous cordwood corpses. She was also the one, of course, who had recommended Simone Weil to Norman in the first place, who besides all her other virtues had engaged in a long spiritual correspondence with a priest, Père Perrin, and once, when we were in Galignani's and saw a biography of

Edith Stein on the table with a picture of a very Jewish-looking nun on the cover, Erika snatched it up with such a hoarse loud laugh of triumph that everybody turned to look at us. She even used phrases like "little Jew" speaking of one of Kaplan's friends, who was evidently even a notch lower than a Viennese handkisser—though actually poor Kaplan turned out to be a Czech. "Norman, she shouldn't say 'little Jew.'" "So tell her." "Erika, you shouldn't say 'little Jew.' It sounds horribly anti-Semitic." She gave me a look of utter surprise and barked with laughter, and I realized that of course she was an expert on anti-Semitism too.

It was the *friend* who fascinated me, of course. Not that I ever saw much of Mme. Meyer, it was hard for her to get away from that government bureau—I never did find out which one. And not that I have any precise memories of our meetings. No, it was their atmospheric quality that made them so lovely, the sight of Mme. Meyer waiting for us at lunchtime in full Paris sunlight on the steps of the Orangerie, at the pier of the bateaux mouches, always in that same outfit that was so utterly Parisian to me: the gray tailleur, and the velvet toque, and the furpiece under the chin, the black kid gloves and dotted veil. Often Norman and Erika would walk on ahead, Erika gesticulating, Norman nodding gravely, and she and I would be left behind, the least of the four as it were, though we didn't mind, sharing a fraught and beautiful silence, smiling at each other charmingly from time to time, even a trifle bored. Then Erika would turn around to point out another obvious landmark, ". . . regardez, le pont Alexandre III . . . ça, c'est le petit arc," emphasis on *petit*, meaning not the Arc de Triomphe, and Mme. Meyer would smile again and nod, not even catching my eye. She was better than anyone I had ever met about being told what she already knew. Sometimes I found myself dying to confide in her, tell her all my fears and yearnings, my feeling for Paris, how it *killed* me to think that next year at that time I would probably be typing for a publisher. How the passing of each summer day, chilly as they were—Paris was actually always damp and cold; each morning I awoke with a wracking cough, fancying myself tubercular—how the passing of each such precious summer day made me ache with nostalgia in advance, like the sight of the lovely marronniers along the Champs-Elysées, already turning copper-colored, like a dying September. ("Exhaust fumes, petite," Erika said, and Norman said, "Exhaust fumes.") But it was all such a cliché emotionally, so embarrassingly much what I assumed Mme. Meyer also knew without being told, that I never said a word to her. Oh, never mind, I'm in *Paris*, I told myself, *Paris*, and the minute I was alone again, slipped off into a patisserie to buy a madeleine to dip into my tea, though they were disappointingly bland in taste, almost like social tea biscuits. What I really loved were the tiny exquisite glazed fruit tartes, fraises, mirabelles, abricots, which I ate sitting outside on a stone bench in the Tuileries, savoring each bite, sweetly and madly in love with all the beauty around me, trying to capture any way I could—I had lately bought some watercolors—the flutter of a leaf through a marble balustrade, formal geometric flower beds in gravel paths, fin de siècle children at play along the rim of the lake, poking little sailboats with their sticks, racing hoops, that painter's blue sky overhead. "The Impressionists invented nothing, merely copied," I wrote in my cahier. "Paris in the sun does shimmer like a Monet. (Manet?) In the rain, it's black and white, like a photograph of itself." Was this right, though? Wouldn't the city shimmer in the rain? Oh, there must be something more, I thought, getting up, brushing off crumbs, taking a bus over to the American Express, hanging out the back. (Another nylon stocking from my parents, it had been days. Also a note from a Mr. Sy Rudnick at the Hôtel Meurice, saying he would be glad to see what he could do for me by way of a broadtail jacket. Randolph was still in analysis and had now discovered he was once in love with me.) There had to be something more. Somebody knew somebody who had been smart enough to buy a delicatessen in Rome, I was doing a project about expatriate writers in Paris and there weren't any, Johnny had discovered he wasn't an Arab, Morty had come all the way to write about his mother in the Bronx, Bobby thought we were all adolescents. Okay, also true that Morty was sometimes taken for a provincial Frenchman by actual Frenchmen, but that still wasn't enough. Not *enough* . . . !

Once Mme. Meyer and I did see each other alone, but it was only for a few minutes, at a little Russian restaurant, her suggestion, where we were all to meet for lunch. Norman and Erika were late, on account of having gone to see Kaplan—and she and I were early. She was already sitting on a red velvet banquette in the corner when I came in, being hovered over by a waiter in a Russian blouse and shaking her head, smilingly, no. I think there was also balalaika music in the background, but the place was dim, and the atmosphere was altogether French. It took her a moment to see me, and then she smiled and reached up and undid her veil, folding it neatly beside her on top of her pocketbook, a very sweet way of getting down to business. We ordered, vodka and black olives, her idea, and then, smiling awkwardly on account of being profile to profile, began to talk of this and that, I saying "Really? How wonderful," during the pauses, as I always did with older women I admired but didn't have much to say to. Then, to fill up one of the silences, I asked her if she had known Erika long.

"Oh, yes," she said, laughing. "We were childhood friends. We were always in and out of each other's houses and playing tricks at school. She used to dip my braids in the inkwell."

It was hard to imagine them sharing the same childhood at all, much less Erika dipping braids into inkwells—though I could hear that laugh, the merry pranks of Till Eulenspiegel. In fact, it was even harder than to imagine Erika in bed with either of the two husbands.

"But then," Mme. Meyer said, still laughing, "she became a genius and left us behind, as we all knew she would."

"Oh, you mustn't say that," I said.

"Say what?"

"That she left you behind."

"But it's true," she said, lifting her delicate half-moon eyebrows above the rimless eyeglasses. Which it was. I felt like an idiot and maybe to make me feel less like one, Mme. Meyer began to tell me more about their implausible youth together, and how their families had known each other for years and years and so on, and then told me a funny story about her own engagement and how when she was visiting her fiancé, her future mother-in-law used to make her sleep in the same bed with her and hold Mme. Meyer's hand tightly all night for good measure.

"She never thought of the afternoon," Mme. Meyer said, turning to me, musing, still amused. And then she kind of woke up and laughed.

The velvet toque with the flower petals turned out to be a hand-me-down from one of the Rothschilds.

"Of course," Erika said, with one of those dreadful barking laughs. "She's an old friend of theirs. What did you think—her name was always *Meyer*?" pronouncing it Mayer, meaning almost but not quite little Jew, the husband was still a German after all, and told me what Charlotte's name had been, which I didn't catch because it meant nothing to me, but seemed to be in the general area of Buddenbrooks, assimilated Jewish version, with generations of philosophers, poets, statesmen and musicians on every hand, and branches in both Germany and France. Actually, we were on our way to Mme. Meyer's house for tea, and since I'd never been invited to a French home before—"She's German," Norman said—I was terribly excited when we followed Erika down into the Métro at L'Odéon and terribly disappointed when, having made about six correspondances, we followed her up out of it at Clamart, which turned out to be a deadly flat brown suburb, silent and still, completely Sunday in the Bronx except that the signs said "tabac" and "boulangerie" instead of "delicatessen." It was the first part of Paris that had ever failed to entice me. The apartment house where Mme. Meyer lived was a couple of blocks away, a dismal chipped tan building with a small grillwork elevator that we crowded into, slowly creaking up five long étages and lurching to a halt at the sixième. Actually, Bobby's landlady lived in a house like this. Mme. Meyer herself opened the door, gaily smiling as usual, but otherwise unfamiliar-looking in a stout blue print silk dress with short sleeves and self-belt buckled around her middle, the kind of dress that Jewish dentists buy for their aging mothers. Without the charm of toque and veil and furpiece, her face looked a bit too square and fleshy, her rimless eyeglasses too severe. They were the eyeglasses of a French schoolteacher in the provinces, the eyeglasses of a Marie-Claire.

Her husband and sister were waiting for us inside, in a small dark salon that was quite overpowered by the usual heavy mahogany refugee furniture, including one of those ubiquitous armoires that they all seemed to have decided to rescue first—even Erika had one crammed into her little apartment over the garage—and which I couldn't understand how they had managed to get past border guards, barking dogs and so on, carrying them on their backs I always somehow imagined, until they had reached the comparative safety of a Clamart, or Washington Heights. All in all, I must confess it was a ghastly visit. The husband was detestable, a fat bristling type with a walrus mustache, who fancied himself an expert on everything—was *this* the charmer Mme. Meyer had to be forcibly restrained from sleeping with? ("A typical *besser wisser*," Erika said, shaking her head over him afterwards, then pausing to instruct us in the phrase, which meant somebody who thought he knew better than anyone else, and blissfully unaware that she was describing herself exactly.) The sister looked like Alice B. Toklas, skinny, shabby, frightened, with straight black hair and bangs. Maybe if the walls had been hung with early Picassos, Matisses, and Braques . . . but there were just a dull flowered wallpaper and a few prints, from that downstairs lobby in the Louvre, I supposed, including a framed detail from Leonardo's "Saint Anne" over the sofa, with those three generations, two women and a baby, sitting on each other's laps, the middle one looking strangely like me. We had tea and some pretty little cakes which Mme. Meyer served us from a shiny glass and chrome tea cart, and M. Meyer, who said he had been a professor of philosophy—Erika raised a wry eyebrow—but was now reduced to teaching ignoramuses and ingrates at a local lycée, told us how when they had first arrived in Paris, he and Mme. Meyer and her sister had sat evening after evening at their dining-room table addressing labels for a few francs apiece. It was a bitter story and he looked at us with bitter scorn when he told it, as if like those "courants d'air" it was all our fault, though he clearly resented the indignity much more on his own behalf than for his wife and sister-in-law. Then he leaned over and fondled the big German shepherd dog at his feet, watching with pleasure when it got up and loped around, scaring us to death. At one point the beast came over and put its paws on Erika's shoulders, face close to hers in what must have been a terrifying searching embrace, though I must say that Erika merely removed the paws firmly one by one, and gave the husband a look, just a look. I sidestepped the beast and went to the w.c. to sort of wash up and collect myself, and couldn't believe my eyes at first when I looked down at the sink and realized that the faucets were German also. *W* and *K*. "Warm und kalt." What an incredible man to have taken his faucets into exile with him also. Weren't the ugly armoire, the Auschwitz beast reminders enough of his past glories? When I came back the atmosphere was even more strained than before, everybody stiff as relatives paying a Sunday call: M. Meyer making some joke about the stupidity of women, the sister mute and wet-eyed in her corner, rough hands folded in a plain cotton lap, Norman bored and beautiful, looking down through his thick black eyelashes at the beret he was swinging between his knees, Erika with her lips tightly closed over her horse-teeth (actually, I almost had to hand it to that husband for being able to make her shut up), Mme. Meyer too readily smiling, too pink, too composed in her Gertz's housedress. It was the one time I was disappointed in her. Foolish, lovely lady to let herself be trapped in that Bronx apartment with that ghastly twosome, though being a great lady she never let on to us that it cost her any emotional pain at all. But why do it? For the sake of old love, old loyalties, old family ties? Or, more probably, because she really was a great lady, the kind who spills wine at her table so you won't feel bad about having spilled yours—though it was difficult to imagine Mme. Meyer making a guest so nervous in the first place. The only thing that was exactly right, that was parfaitement Mme. Meyer chez soi as I had envisioned it, was the glistening tea cart with its silver pot and china cups and pretty little cakes, puffs and tarts, exquisite, each with its tiny slice of blue plum, glazed peach.

"No, thank you, madame," I said when, following my gaze, she charmingly offered me another. "But they're lovely. Exquisite."

The husband snorted. It was the ugly, skinny sister who had made them.

"A typical *besser wisser*," Erika repeated, as we emerged from the Métro at Odéon again and continued on to the Deux Magots where Norman had arranged a kind of symposium for her among our friends, and paused once more to give us a little lesson in the phrase, though I must say her open dislike of M. Meyer puzzled me. Not that he wasn't perfectly awful, he was: though frankly much more Erika's type than that sweet dippy invalid back in Gorham, who was going to bring us all the new humanism, starting with Gorham—no, Wheaton. Still, usually Erika never brooked *any* criticism of *anything* pertaining to herself, which ought to have included not only Charlotte Meyer but the husband also. Maybe it was just that the visit to the Meyer household seemed to have brought us together, as if, like Desdemona and Othello, we now loved each other for the dangers we had passed and that we did pity them. In fact, I hardly even minded when about two minutes after we had entered the café, several marble tables had already been pushed together and we were all sitting around them in a rigid semicircle, Norman saying, naturally: "—and not only *that*, Erika, but also—" Still, considering her initial reluctance to meet our friends at all—"Oh, come now, Norman, look here!"—it was amazing how quickly Erika warmed up to the occasion, and how by the time the garçon had finished plunking down our tiny coffees and the apéritifs on the old Hemingway saucers, she had already managed to give us the lowdown on nylon underwear, avoid, too cold in the winter, too hot in the summer, the superiority of Bufferin over aspirin, the fact that no one but a German could possibly conduct Beethoven, and advised us all to stay away from our parents, Morty Cohen nodded knowingly, mothers especially, Morty Cohen nodded in dead earnest. ("Are you sure you're not just being bitchy?" Norman said to me later, claiming not to have heard. "Are you sure she didn't just mean yours?") Then there was the usual pause, and we all sipped and smiled awkwardly at each other, and looked to see who was coming in the door, which happened to be what looked like a typical American tourist, blond, crew-cut, camera-laden, and whom Erika indicated to us all with a knowing tilt of the head and a short derisive laugh. Actually, I thought it might be Henri Cartier-Bresson, but nobody else seemed to notice because they were all listening to Erika again, who was now asking everybody what they did. Johnny just gave her the old nervous yukking laugh, and Morty made a few gracefully modest allusions to a work in progress. Then Marie-Claire, with her usual air of sullen defiance, said that when the fight against the capitalist oppressors was won maybe then she would have time to return to her own selfish aims and ambitions, and Elaine Cohen, the only one of us with an actual job, come to think of it, said she worked for the U.S. Embassy, and kept smiling brightly and eagerly at Marie-Claire to take the sting off it. Bobby came last, stammering out his ambition to be a conductor, at which Erika nodded, informing him never to be misled into believing that Toscanini could do justice to Beethoven and also, through some logical step I couldn't quite follow, that the *Zauberflöte* was Mozart's best opera. A legitimate opinion, though personally my own favorite was *Don Giovanni*, except that what Erika loved about the *Zauberflöte* was the libretto. Ha, ha, that Papageno! A great loud bark that made Bobby spit up a bit of his coffee. By now I was almost positive it was Henri Cartier-Bresson, but still no one noticed, not even Marie-Claire, who was at that moment being advised by Erika to read the fiction of Mary McCarthy if she truly wanted to understand the social scene in the United States. "*Mary McCarthy?*" Of all the women to admire, of all the writers, why *that* one? "Americans don't understand the genre, petite," Erika said to me, smiling kindly all around, and also admitting a little later on that Mary McCarthy was a great admirer of *hers*. "What do you think of Faulkner?" Johnny said, with a painful grinning show of his big white teeth. Another genre of which Erika approved but Americans couldn't possibly appreciate. "He's too metaphysical for them," Erika explained to Johnny gently. "Johnny's an American," I said to Morty. "Shsh," Morty said, smiling and putting a hand on my arm, and then out loud confessed himself guilty of a, perhaps, finer, possibly, more personal appreciation of Henry James—a graceful pause, assuming graceful agreement—and then continued with some elaborate, practically baroque allusions to *The Wings of the Dove*, and the Princess Casamassima and Roderick Hudson (I think he also threw in a few words about omelettes aux fines herbes and aerial perspective)—and ended by asking Erika how she was finding Paris and expressing the hope that she was amusing herself well? "Look here, my friend," Erika said, hooting with laughter, "I already found Paris when you were in diapers," an unfortunate figure of speech considering the nature of Morty's work-in-progress, though Morty took it well, smiling graciously as if they had just engaged in a charming jeu de mots. And Erika continued of *course* she loved Paris, how could she *not* love Paris, particularly since in addition to the discomfort of the clammy nylon underwear, nothing smelled in America, not even the strawberries. And, naturally, Marie-Claire had to tell how she had blasphemed with that coke on top of the Milan Cathedral, though to my amazement Erika listened with great and serious interest, with a look like Norman's when he and Marie-Claire shook hands, nodding thoughtfully, lips importantly brought together over those long juicy teeth.

A long lonesome lull came over us. Outside night had fallen, and the inside of the Deux Magots was now lit up like a Lautrec. We all ordered more drinks with the Hemingway saucers, including Kenny Schwartz, who was up from Aix-en-Provence to visit Bobby and had just come over to our pushed-together tables. Sotto voce, Bobby tried to cadge a few francs from him and failed. Then Elaine asked Erika about her travel plans—we were always asking about travel plans when these long lonesome lulls came over us, and making ourselves even more lonesome. Erika paused, one of the few times I had ever known her to pause before an answer, and said things had come up— but after Paris and the Cultural Congress she would probably visit Jaspers in Basel (or was it Heidegger in Bonn?). Kenny Schwartz, long-nosed and pimpled, asked her in his innocence if she had any plans to go to Israel. This time Erika literally did roar with laughter, like a Santa Claus in a German Macy's, with all these great Prussian "Ho ho's" resounding all over the place. "Mon vieux, I couldn't go to Israel even if I wanted to." "She's on the blacklist of the Irgun," Norman said proudly, like a fight manager, alluding to Erika's most recent article for *Commonwealth* on the plight of the Arab refugees, an article that not only had the Irgun but practically the whole of the B'nai B'rith gunning for her. It was another puzzling case of intellectual cachet, like Dietrich Bonhoeffer. *I* was worried about the plight of the Arab refugees too, who wouldn't be? But I still couldn't understand what made it intellectually more elevated than worrying about the Israelis. ". . . I do have a certain admiration for Carson McCullers," Marie-Claire said, operating on some depressed wavelength of her own, as usual. Again Erika listened with surprising respect. "Yes, it's amazing that one so young should understand so much." So naturally poor dopey Bobby had to go and tell her that *all* Americans were adolescent. This time Erika gave such a great hoot of laughter, it broke up the meeting, though I wasn't sure whether it was because she agreed with him, or found it so absurd that somebody as little and nervous and sweaty and dopey as Bobby should imagine himself entitled to such an opinion.

As we walked her back to her hotel, all my good feelings toward Erika had vanished—what a bitch, really—leaving in their wake a kind of insane tenderness toward Bobby, even though only last week when Bobby and I went to see *Le Dindon* at the Comédie Française together—neither Norman's French nor his tastes inclined toward the Comédie—I had laughed too and pushed him away when Bobby tried to kiss me good-bye afterward, and laughed again when he looked up and said, "Don't be coy." But that wasn't the point. It was like those Yankee-Go-Home signs, like when she was being bitchy to Norman. Though I must say, at the moment she was clinging to his arm like a spent actress, putting on the same great show of intellectual exhaustion as she did after the seminars in Gorham, when she practically staggered out of the classroom, palm to forehead. Norman gently and timidly asked if maybe she would like to come up and see our rooms, a suggestion I expected her to wave off, as usual, as if the very idea were beneath contempt. But instead she said, "Certainly, mon chou." We made a detour over to the rue de la Harpe, escorting her quickly past the patron, who was waiting for customers at his usual station in the doorway, wearing a striped shirt with sleeve garters and a collar button but no collar, and climbed up the six flights, Erika without a murmur of complaint. In fact she was quite extravagant with her "merveilleux's" and kept pointing out the extraordinary cleanliness of the place, which fortunately she seemed to assume she was bringing to my attention for the first time.

"Mais, c'est vraiment merveilleux!" Erika exclaimed again, after we had poked our heads into my room and then gone to sit in Norman's, which was almost the same as mine but larger: maroon velvet portières, dim rose-colored light in the ceiling that went off when you put on the one over the bed. "How did you find it, kinder?"

"Sonia found it actually," Norman said, giving my head a proprietary pat, and then opened the French windows, which he never did, and stepped out on the balcony to show her the view.

"Really, petite?" Erika said, sinking into a faded red velvet armchair instead of following. "I'm impressed that you know your way around Paris so well," and then, in a lower voice and a conspiratorial inclination of the head toward Norman out there, "—how long have you two been together?"

Quotes on "together." It sounded wonderfully European.

"—about ten months."

"Oh? Ce n'était pas arrivé à Gorham?"

"No, we kind of came 'together' on the boat train."

Erika nodded, with the kind impersonality of a lady gynecologist. "Ten months. At your age that's a long time, petite. Try not to break up with him. At this stage a break would kill him."

"What about me?" I said, laughing, and Erika impatiently waved me aside, which ought to have been insulting but wasn't. We both looked at Norman, silhouetted on the balcony against a dark Paris sky, arm outstretched in a "—and not only *that*" kind of gesture, pointing out the Boul' Mich.

"—Erika, is it hard to cook?" I said, not knowing why the question had come to mind, except that I had suddenly remembered that once, after a very little "little evening" she had served these delicious Königsberger klops, followed by a dessert of rote grütze.

"Hard to cook? Of course not," Erika said.

"No, but I mean—how long would it take to make a normal dinner, for instance?"

Erika shrugged. "Thirty minutes. Forty minutes." She paused a moment, and then nodded, agreeing with herself. "No, there's absolutely no reason to spend more than forty minutes in the kitchen. Also be sure he wipes and puts away afterward, pots too."

"Really?" I said.

"Absolutely."

Norman climbed back in from the balcony and we both looked at him blankly. He looked back at us blankly too, having just realized we had never been out there. Erika stayed only a few minutes more, just long enough to look over the top of the pile of yellow books on Norman's night table, all with titles like *Gestalt of Etwas* and the *Untergeschichte of* something else, approve, tell Norman to "—look *here*, Norman," a few times, distribute a few more "merveilleux's" to the room in general and laughingly shake her head to the offer of a glass of the wine we bought by the litre. In fact, she was meeting Mme. Meyer for a late dinner. She headed for the door, smoothing down her white gloves and pulling the loose tweed coat more tightly around her. Underneath, her dress had been a navy blue silk that was a kind of sister to Mme. Meyer's floral print from Gertz (to be factual, probably the Galeries Lafayette), except that Erika's bosom, though large too, was completely concave and schoolteachery.

"Listen, kinder," she said casually, pausing with her hand on the door handle. "I need your advice."

Advice? The word from Erika's lips was so completely unexpected, that I almost missed hearing the problem, which was merely that she had just received a letter from an old uncle asking her to cut short her stay in Paris and come to Königsberg for her aunt's birthday. It was to be a big sentimental celebration, with all the survivors of the family who could possibly make it attending. A cousin from Israel was coming too.

"So, tell me, kinder, what must I do?" Erika said, sighing. "Yield to the wishes of this old man whom I never even cared for in the old days, or ignore him and stay in Paris until the eighteenth as I planned?"

"If you went, when would you have to go?" Norman said anxiously.

"Tuesday, at the absolute latest."

"But that's so soon. You only just got here."

"I know, Norman, I know," Erika said sympathetically, though both of them were pretty far from the truth. She'd been around for weeks. "But look here, they are the only ones left, and I must go to Germany in any case."

It was all so puzzling. A cousin from Israel—what if he belonged to the Irgun? And what about all the advice to avoid our families at all costs?

"Listen, Erika, the hell with Germany," I said impetuously, "the hell with your family—" and then, since she seemed less surprised by my outburst than I was, and in fact seemed to be taking it kindly, I even put my arm around her and jollied her up a bit. "Oh, you know what I mean. Stay in Paris with us and with your friend. We'll have fun."

"It's not that easy, petite," Erika said, laughing.

"Yes, I know, but—"

"Petite, I must go now," she said, touching my cheek with a gloved hand, and letting herself out the door. "Thank you for letting me intrude."

I walked her as far as the stairwell, calling "au revoir" and "à bientôt" as I watched her descend a few flights. Two Arabs in raincoats and naked legs pressed themselves against the wall to let her go by, and I hoped that our skinny, limping chambermaid with the fever spots on her cheeks wouldn't suddenly start rushing around with a vacuum cleaner and an armful of sheets. When I went back inside, Norman was sitting on the bed, busily slitting page after page of *La Pesanteur et la Grâce*, and stopping only to knock back a couple of Bufferin for what was evidently a fresh headache. He never used water and so it involved some rather hard gulps and swallows.

"Actually, she's kind of touching, isn't she?" I said, when he was finished. "Gallant almost, in a unique kind of way."

"You don't think that perhaps you were a bit cavalier about sending her family and all of Germany to hell?" Norman said, continuing the busywork with the paper slitter, and breathing just a bit harder through his handsome Jewish nostrils. I hadn't expected him to understand, in fact I had known his agitation over her leaving would override all finer feeling.

"Darling, don't worry," I said, sitting down on the bed beside him. "Even if she goes on Tuesday, she's scheduled to be back in August. I was just trying to reassure her, that's all, make her feel wanted. I don't think you realize how unsure of herself she is fundamentally under that rigid façade, how lonely. I mean, she's really just as human as the rest of us, don't you see? Family driving her nuts—"

"Don't make her *that* human," Norman said.

"Norman, it is not an insult to a person to call them human. On the contrary, it's a compliment, a form of welcome to the entire race." I got up. "—Anyway, I do feel sorry for her."

"Why?" Norman said.

"Because, my love, the truth isn't ugly. It's beautiful."

I looked at him sitting there, more depressed and anxious than ever, and headed for the little wrought iron balcony. "Oh, why is it always Simone Weil?" I said. "I love Colette. Why aren't there ever any points for her?"

* * *

For her last day in Paris, Erika decreed a last visit to the Louvre, which I certainly would have excused myself from if I hadn't been so sure it *was* her last day: not at all to my surprise, she had accepted the invitation to the old uncle's birthday party in Königsberg, though naturally putting it on some elevated intellectual basis, nothing involving the German equivalent of candles and cake. I had always hated going to museums with other people anyway, a problem traveling around Europe, even without Erika. It spoiled the pictures, and instead of seeing them, I would wind up staring blankly and telling myself how artistic I was. Also we had been hard at it for some time, and my feet hurt from the long beautiful polished parquet floors. I longed to go back to the Hôtel de la Harpe and soak them in the bidet. I stopped where I was, in front of my favorite Bronzino, the beautiful young boy in black suit and ruff, and let Erika and Norman and Mme. Meyer continue to clatter on ahead down the long Galerie d'Apollon, three figures diminishing in perspective, surrounded by heavy, gold-framed paintings as far up as the domed and gilded ceiling, and Erika's increasingly tiny index finger pointing out one and then another. Nevertheless, I had to admit that, for Erika, she was acting pretty subdued, though I wasn't sure whether it was the prospect of leaving that had softened her up around the edges or whether, having finished with us small potatoes, she was now saving her intellectual fire for Jaspers in Basel and Heidegger in Bonn. To say nothing of that international Cultural Congress. I turned back to my Bronzino and realized suddenly how much he resembled Norman: beautiful, full-lipped, serious, curly-haired, reproachful—though of course Norman wasn't walleyed—and then absently wandered on to "La Gioconda," a painting I frankly detested and that it irked me to have to move closer to in order to avoid my reflection in her protective glass.

"But what do you want to be inscrutable *for*, Mona?" I said, irritated by the petty meanness of those narrowed eyes, the tiny grudging smile, the pederastic smell of the bitch. Yes, there was a distinct aroma of Gide about her, though she also curiously reminded me of a girl I had once gone to sleep-away camp with who was always running off

into the bushes with the boys. I backed away, and in doing so realized I had gradually been encircled by a crowd of tourists, the usual
international bunch, family types saying "oh and ah" in their various
languages, "formidable," "épatant," "carina," "ach wie schön," plus that
sudden sharp intake of the breath that Germans use for *yes*! I looked
around, and of course the emphatic breather was Erika, who gave me
a short nod of recognition before she pursed her lips and studied the
painting some more, finally nodding and sucking in her breath again,
as if she had just given Leonardo her final seal of approval, which was
the sort of thing only Erika could do without any self-consciousness
or compunction at all. Mme. Meyer was proceeding on to the next
gallery, with Norman looking stiff and unlikely but kind of sweet
beside her, so that evidently Erika had come back expressly to fetch
me, which was very flattering, more flattering than I liked to admit. I
didn't even feel called upon to comment on the painting.

". . . Paris, Paris," Erika said with one of her weightier sighs, speaking to me, though she kept her eyes fixed on "La Gioconda." "I envy
you, petite, for being able to stay."

"Well, must you go?" I said, turning to her with a sudden feeling
of tenderness, and had to remind myself that I was always moved by
anything that was coming to an end, and had even cried at Pier 91 saying good-bye to my brother-in-law, Irving. Nevertheless, the woman
was even wearing the exact same outfit in which she'd arrived, much
the worse for wear now, little navy blue straw hat askew on those aging
Weimar Republic curls, ears popping out in between, pale tweed coat
falling back off her shoulders.

"*Must* you go?" I repeated.

"Norman showed me one of your little watercolors," Erika said to
"La Gioconda." "*Pas mal.*"

". . . I don't do them seriously," I said, after a moment, also to "La
Gioconda." "Just for my own pleasure."

"That's obvious. Still, I'm impressed that one so young can see so
much."

"Only young people see what young people see," I said, irritated by
the paraphrase about Carson McCullers. I wasn't Marie-Claire, after
all. "There's nothing to be impressed about."

"Ho, ho!" Erika cried, erupting into that nerve-shattering Prussian Santa Claus laugh of hers, which had made poor Bobby choke and spit up his coffee at the Deux Magots. "And what does a child like *you* think she knows?"

For the first time I wished we were back in the United States, where museums were still hushed and reverential and a guard would have come rushing over to make her shut up. But being, as we were, in the midst of a crowd of tourists parading up and down, Venetian style, male Italians, fat disgusting Germans in their fat disgusting lederhosen, skinny pinched French, we could just as well have been two more pigeons flapping away at the Piazza San Marco. I looked toward the far end of the gallery where Mme. Meyer was making a discreet ladylike exit with a hand on Norman's arm, somehow transforming him into a gentleman.

"She likes you, petite," Erika said.

"Really? Well, I like *her*," I said, not sorry to have had my mind read.

"And *trusts* you," Erika added, impervious to my thin little shaft of malice. She gave a conspiratorial look all around, and in spite of myself, I did too.

"Look, petite," Erika said to me eye to eye again, woman to woman. "To tell you the truth, I'm worried about her."

"Worried?"

". . . she didn't tell you about the suicide?" Erika said, glancing away.

"*Suicide? Whose* suicide?"

"It's all *right*, petite," Erika said, turning back to me and laughing indulgently, a mother to an idiot child. "Nothing *happened*. . . ." But the laugh lacked its usual force, and as it faded, for the first time I saw Erika look frankly worried. "—look, petite, I want you to keep an eye on her for me while I'm gone. I'm not sure what she'll do next."

Do next? I didn't even know what Mme. Meyer had done in the first place.

"It was the week before I came," Erika said. "She wandered around all night with that gun in her pocketbook."

"*Gun?*"

"Thank god she never found the courage to use it," Erika said, shaking her head. "It was still in her lap when the flics found her sitting in the Tuileries at dawn."

The *police* accosting Mme. Meyer at dawn? "Erika, I don't understand. Are you trying to tell me Mme. Meyer tried to kill herself? Why would she want to kill herself?"

"She adored him," Erika said, shrugging, and caught herself and looked at me again, "—you mean she didn't tell you about the lover, either?"

"She didn't tell me anything," I said, wishing that damn Mona Lisa would stop smiling and look ambiguous again.

"Never mind," Erika said. "The details don't matter. She's not the first woman in the world to be deserted by a man and she won't be the last. In fact, if not for that miserable ménage à trois situation at home, I wouldn't even be concerned at all."

"*Ménage à trois?*"

"Oh, ma petite," Erika said, "surely you realized that Charlotte and her husband and her sister—" and was about to break into that unnerving bark of laughter again, when this time *I* looked around like a detective, and so did she, and closed her eyes, and shook her head, hat and all, and sighed, as if she were remembering for the very last time that nothing *smelled* in America.

"Okay," Erika said, all business again. "Now, listen, petite. Now you understand why I've had to keep postponing my departure. And why I'm so worried about her. And why I'm depending on *you*, little one, to keep an eye on her for me. She swears she won't try anything again, but who knows—?" I don't think she actually clasped me by the shoulder at that moment, but it certainly felt like it. "—and, remember, not a word about this to anyone, not even Norman. Men don't understand these things."

True. Neither did I—*me* keep an eye on Mme. Meyer?—though I could hardly press the point since Lady Charlotte and Norman had just strolled back into the gallery looking for us. Inevitably, I had expected her to look all gray and haggard and the very familiarity of her gay pink face with the French maquillage took me by surprise. It would need some adjusting to. Then Erika said, giving me a quick meaning look, enough pictures, kinder, time for tea, and we set out across the long courtyard of the Louvre in a fine gray drizzle. As usual I found myself paired off with Mme. Meyer, only, for the first time since we'd met I felt uneasy in her presence and kept looking at her sideways whenever she lifted her veil to dab at the moisture inside her eyeglasses—what was she wiping off with that dainty handkerchief, rain or tears? Then a couple of times she smiled at me, gold tooth radiant in the back, and I gave her a dismal smile in return, finding her somewhat shorter than usual, trying not to remember that behind this infinite gray prison/palace courtyard were the gardens of the Tuileries where leaves fluttered through marble balustrades and suicidal ladies were discovered at dawn by friendly flics and escorted home by the elbow. Why all the smiles, anyway? Was she happy again, was she just seeking to console me for the terrible things she sensed I now knew about her? It was a case for Morty Cohen, for Henry James, not for me. No, I thought, no, my god, it wasn't *possible* that this lovely lady had been wandering about Paris all night with a gun. Where would she get a gun? Why would she want the mess of using it? And what about that ménage à trois? How could she get herself to climb into bed with that obnoxious husband in the first place, much less with that Alice B. Toklas sister clambering in on the other side? *Which* side? Oh, my god. No, no, not this lovely lady, not this charmer in the toque and veil sailing alongside me like a ship with ample prow, like my nice aunt if I had a nice aunt. I knew this was stupid. I knew it was gauche by every standard of psychology and literature, but I couldn't help it. I looked around for Norman, who was bringing up the rear, wanting to entangle my arm with his, press and hook myself into the warm physical fact of his presence. But he had already gone ahead, eager to catch up with his Erika, who was striding along, shoulders back, chin up, navy blue straw hat and veil askew but clinging tenaciously to her head. With one white-gloved hand she held fast to her pocketbook. The other, she had cupped to catch the rain.

The rain, the rain, the rain, retreat from Caporetto, a farewell to arms. I knew I was being obsessive but I couldn't help it. I couldn't get the dear ruin of Mme. Meyer out of my mind: the rimless eyeglasses splattered like mournful windshields, the drooping shoulders, the clotted furpiece. I tasted my couscous oriental and choked, having put in too much pepper sauce, in spite of all of Morty's warnings right from the beginning never to confuse it with gravy, and wished I were safely upstairs in my room at the Hôtel de la Harpe, instead of in this Balkan restaurant next door where we always ate when the weather was bad, and which I usually loved on account of its crowded cheap spicy smells, and its openness to the street like a Near Eastern food bazaar. But tonight the wet wind was ruffling the corners of the paper couverts where the waiter had just scribbled the cost of our prix-fixe and demi-carafe of rouge, and we kept needing to hold them down. Also, the weird character who sometimes haunted the place was back again, never eating, just watching us all from against the rear wall: a young man dressed in Napoleonic style but all in black, black tricorn hat, black ruffled cape mildewed around the edges, black trousers, his face pale and greenish, as if he had been floating underwater a long time. I remembered how Morty had laughed knowingly the first time I had described this apparition, called him "ce type," explained that he considered himself the last of the Bonapartists, so that I had immediately entered in my graph-paper cahier my first encounter with a true eccentric of Paris. But tonight he was eerie watching us, deathlike, a real ghost. Also, the conversation with Erika about cooking had made me suddenly tired of eating in restaurants, which I had been doing for almost a year. It was lonesome always eating in restaurants. Why didn't the French ever ask you to their homes? Why had it only been Mme. Meyer who, as Norman pointed out, was German anyway?

"Oh, Norman," I said, already torn with guilt about breaking my promise to Erika, but unable to hold back any longer. "Qu'est-ce que tu penses de Mme. Meyer?"

"Why?" Norman said, breaking off a piece of bread and sopping up. "What am I supposed to pense?"

"You're not *supposed* to anything. I just wondered, did you notice anything odd about her?"

"I thought you loved her."

"I did. I do. I was just inquiring if you remarked anything special about her, anything out of the ordinary—?"

"Well, obviously she's a person of extreme intelligence," Norman said. "Otherwise, Erika would hardly—"

I gave it up. Erika was right, men didn't understand such things. But, my God, what if Erika was right about everything? "—listen, she really is leaving tomorrow, isn't she?"

"On the eight o'clock train," Norman said.

I leaned back and poured myself a little more wine from the carafe. Really a rather nice red ordinaire, and probably quite easy on the liver. "I still don't see how she can bring herself to go back there," I said, "even if it is her family."

"She's German."

"She's a German Jew. How can she forget that?"

"She doesn't forget it," Norman said, "she forgives them."

"Oh, *Norman*—"

"You know, you're really getting quite obsessive on the Jewish question," Norman said, reaching for more bread with a strange air of calm. "You really ought to watch it. Bursting into tears that time in Florence—"

"There were only two old people left in the courtyard of that whole huge synagogue. And they were waiting for *soup*!"

"Going to the Rothschild synagogue for both Rosh Hashanah *and* Yom Kippur—" Norman said.

I was about to retort that nevertheless somebody like Mme. Meyer would never be able to bring herself to go back to Germany and the reason I knew was that I once asked her and she said as much. Then a goose walked over my grave and I shivered and quieted down the flapping couvert and shut up. But only for a minute.

"I still wouldn't ever step foot in that country," I said. "*Ever.*"

"So don't."

"Don't worry. I won't."

"Nobody ever asked you to anyway," Norman said, bending over his plate. Emphasis on the *you*.

"Really? Well, it doesn't matter because even if they did—" But no, wait a minute, he wasn't bent over on account of eating. Norman was waiting for a blow to fall.

"*Norman!*"

"It's only for three weeks," Norman said, making himself look up at me again, and forcing a hysterically casual laugh. "—I don't even think I'll bother with Basel."

"Three *weeks*!"

"She said you wouldn't mind."

"Oh, *did* she?"

"Okay," Norman said, shrugging off the dare, "then come with us."

"I'd sooner die first."

"I told you you were being obsessive."

"I'm not obsessive. I'd just have some practical problems with soap and lampshades."

"Oh, Sonia, Sonia," Norman said, "that kind of flippancy is intellectually totally unworthy of you."

"I am not an intellectual, thank God."

"Of course you are. You just spend all your time trying to avoid it."

"Speaking of which—" I said, suddenly putting down my wineglass. "Just how and when *did* the great philosopher see my little '*pas mal*' watercolor?"

"What are you talking about?" Norman said.

"Whose room did you show it to her in, yours or mine?"

Norman shook his head and laughed. I seemed to be surrounded lately by mirthless people who were always laughing. "Listen," he said, putting his hand over mine, "you want to know how off-base you are? I'll tell you something. A long time ago, I did try to sleep with Erika, if you want to know the truth. And you want to know what she did? She laughed and pushed me away."

". . . When?" I said. "When was it?"

"I don't remember," Norman said, frowning and unhanding my hand. "A long time ago. After one of the little evenings. It doesn't matter."

"Did the Schulzes take it all down on the tape recorder?"

"I *told* you—"

"I know. She laughed and pushed you away." No wonder he hadn't wanted to see *Le Dindon*. This boy was already an expert on bedroom farce. "—but who was the joke on, Norman, you or her?"

"Look, I simply refuse to deal with you on that level," Norman said, looking busily around the restaurant, so young and handsome and trapped that I might have felt sorry for him if I hadn't been furious. Then he caught sight of that greenish-white ghost watching us from against the wall and turned back to me again, staring miserably while I stared at him. I gave him the money for my couscous and my half of the demi-carafe, and then we went back to the Hôtel de la Harpe, holding hands all the way up the six flights of stairs and made love silently, in my room, which was like Norman's, but smaller, less cluttered up with books and magazines and papers. Then afterwards, I turned off the rose-colored bulb over the bed that had already extinguished the light in the ceiling—but, oh, how beautiful Norman was when he was sleeping, anxious Jewish curls plastered damply to his forehead, thick black eyelashes, unhealthy white skin, pouting red mouth—and went out onto the balcony like a Balzac hero, looking out over the red and green roofs of Paris, straining to see a last flying buttress of Notre Dame. Down below, on the narrow sidewalk of the rue de la Harpe itself, a few Arabs in pajama tops and skimpy berets were busily palming things off on each other while the patron stood nearby, watching. Then another Arab in a jacket came along leading a kinky-haired young woman in wedgies, and our patron nodded them inside. It took forty-five minutes. I knew because once I happened to be downstairs talking to the chambermaid about the typing paper clipped around Norman's light, and I heard them arranging it. I went back inside and lay down next to Norman, beautiful Norman, already a bit on the fat side, already a tiny bit prematurely bald, as indicated by the high naked peaks of his temples, and took him in my arms, cupping his head closely against mine. Oh, farewell, farewell, my beautiful Bronzino boy, *adieu, adieu, Chéri.* . . . Hello, Aunt Rose's Stanley?

"Norman," I whispered in the darkness, "I have something to tell you too."

"—what?"

"My real name is Sandra."

"Oh, Sonia, Sonia," Norman said, and turned over.

EPILOGUE

There were foreign noises from the other side of the wall in what had been Norman's room, a man's voice joking in French, accordian music on the radio. Outside, the rue de la Harpe was black and wet as night though it was late in the morning, redolent of that dark green bitter smell of Paris that I would know anywhere and that had been stirring me even in my sleep. I lay on my bed eating a dry croissant left over from breakfast, and thinking about Norman last evening at the station, leaning forward toward his Erika in the voiture of their Grand Express Européen, the two of them face-to-face against red velvet and lace antimacassars—Erika had sailed into France cabin class but was going to Germany in first, which meant, yes it had to mean, that she was paying for Norman too—laughing excitedly, those serious laughers, now leaning further forward, knees almost touching, now leaning back, either way terribly anxious to be off. I had brought them a few things for their journey, a Beaujolais recommended by Morty, and some tartes from an elegant patisserie near the Madeleine, by Erika totally unappreciated, though Norman wanted to open the wine right away and was finally prevailed on to just untie the little box of tartes. Mme. Meyer's present was a two-volume Pléiade edition of Michelet's *Histoire de France* which I knew must have cost her about six thousand francs, a sum that being a clerk in that little government bureau, she could hardly have afforded. Leaving the station, I had promised to meet her for lunch today at a little bistro on the rue Monsieur le Prince, an appointment I had no desire to keep and that I knew I would. The runts of the litter, still taking care of each other. It amused me that I was still so carefully obeying Erika's instructions, and that though I obviously didn't know my strength yet, I was getting so awfully familiar with my weaknesses.

There was a timid knock on the door, and our chambermaid, Josette, limped in for my tray, looking more skinny and overworked than ever on account of that red fever spot on each cheek, and rather like Petrouchka, carrying her feather duster like a prop. "Well, Josette," I said, "il n'y a personne ici sauf nous poules," to which she said "Comment?" and limped out again. It was almost time to meet Mme. Meyer anyway. Downstairs I nodded to the patron who, on account of the inclement weather, was waiting for customers *inside* the doorway, but wearing the usual long-sleeved striped shirt with the sleeve garters and collar button but no collar, and then, since I had a few minutes to spare, made a detour over to the quai—the Voltaire, I think, our favorite, the most quietly beautiful—and rested my elbows on the wet stone and looked out, thinking of the night that Norman had hoisted himself up on the parapet, and I had held him there, in between his legs. It had begun to rain again, not a refreshing drenching summer rain, just a fine moisture, enough to dull the mood. I pictured to myself again that Anna Karenina wagon-lit, still romantic and hissing steam, but now about to journey to jagged bombed-out bitter places like Köln, and of Norman saying, rather taken aback, and with a mouth sticky with tart: "Sure—but I thought you wouldn't be caught dead there." Actually in fact, the patron had been very nice about agreeing to let Norman have his room back when he returned, probably still astounded to have tenants who rented by the week instead of by the hour, and, of course, three weeks was hardly a lifetime, not even a season. I reminded myself that it was getting late and that Mme. Meyer was probably already waiting for me in the little bistro on the rue Monsieur le Prince, no doubt already poised to begin the charming business of looking up and smiling when she saw me and reaching behind to untie the dotted veil. Poor desperate creature. Why had Erika told me her story? What kind of a bitch would tell a kid a story like that, anyway? Maybe it wasn't even true. Maybe Erika had just invented it out of jealousy or pique. Or maybe, which would have been really fascinating, maybe it was Mme. Meyer who had lied to Erika. No, more than fascinating, practically Jamesian, the perfect opening to a story by James. Yes, I could imagine myself turning away from the quai and walking slowly and heavy-heartedly over to the restaurant, stopping maybe to read the menu in violet ink that was posted in the window, maybe hesitating in the doorway before I went in. Then there she would be sitting toward the back, at a little table with a red checkered cloth, waiting for me, a lovely veiled lady in a gray tailleur and furpiece, seen through a purplish smoky haze of Gauloise bleu. There would be a bottle of red wine at her elbow, and also on the red checkered cloth, another paper menu written in violet ink. I would slip in beside her, sweetly sad, saddened even more by her charming light chatter, while the waiter returned to pour our wine, serve us our omelettes aux fines herbes from a silver chafing dish. We would eat in silence. And then, putting down her fork, Mme. Meyer would lay a hand over mine, and say with a smiling air of entreaty: "Forgive her, my dear." "Forgive her, Madame? Who? For what?" But shaking her head and still smiling, she would press on: "—and if you can, my dear, do forgive me." Forgive *her*? Forgive her for *what*? . . . And then suddenly the whole world would come alive again and I would *understand*! Because (yes, end on a metaphor), plump and pink as she was, Mme. Meyer would suddenly have made me think of a willow tree. When the wind blew, she would bend with it, pliantly, gracefully, perhaps even touching her head to the ground. But when the wind stopped. . . .

Willow? Were there willows in Paris? Yes, all over the place, in the Bois de Boulogne, dripping over the quais. But why not chestnut? Why not copper beech? Marronnier? And in fact, why would Mme. Meyer have lied? To be kind, of course. Kind to whom? To Erika. To give Erika that juicy morsel of human weakness that people like Erika need to feed on. But why invent such a dreadful lie? Or was the part about the lover and the suicide true, and the rest false? The husband, the sister? The ménage à trois? Oh, accept the ambiguity, Sonia/Sandra, I told myself. Make yourself a present of it. Take it with grace. But I couldn't. I kept my elbows on the wet stone parapet, listening to an occasional clip-clop behind me and looking out over the Seine. On the other side of the quai, a row of crumbling old buildings stood very still, black and white, waiting to be photographed. A few wisps of smoke straggled out of slippery chimneys. Below, the red and green roofs glistened and undulated in black water. Then, presently a coal barge came sliding silently along, ducking under the bridge with its fin de siècle lampposts, and gliding on, until it became a toy boat in the distance and ceased to exist. Oh, I'm in *Paris*, I told myself passionately, *Paris*! And then, being still young, I put down my head, and cried.

Lightning Source UK Ltd.
Milton Keynes UK
UKHW010805030621
384862UK00001B/120